Resisting HER

...ll Ryan is the *New York Times* and *USA Today* bestselling
...r of contemporary romance novels, including *Hard to Love,*
...*vel Me, Resisting Her* and the *Filthy Beautiful Lies* series.

...s a sassy, yet polite Midwestern girl with a deep love of
...oks, and a slight addiction to lipgloss. She lives in
...nneapolis with her adorable husband and two baby sons,
... cooking, hiking, being active, and reading. Find
... at www.kendallryanbooks.com

Also by Kendall Ryan

Filthy Beautiful series
Filthy Beautiful Lies
Filthy Beautiful Love
Filthy Beautiful Lust
Filthy Beautiful Forever

Unravel Me series
Unravel Me
Make Me Yours

Love by Design series
Working It
Craving Him
All or Nothing

When I Break series
When I Break
When I Surrender
When We Fall

Hard To Love
Resisting Her
The Impact of You

Resisting HER

Kendall Ryan

HARPER

Harper
An imprint of HarperCollins*Publishers*
1 London Bridge Street
London SE1 9FG

www.harpercollins.co.uk

A Paperback Original 2015
1

A catalogue record for this book
is available from the British Library

ISBN: 978-0-00-813406-8

Set in Minion by Born Group using Atomik ePublisher from Easypress

MIX
**Paper from
responsible sources**

FSC
www.fsc.org   FSC™ C007454

Prologue

Cole listened to the soft sounds of her breathing, wondering how he'd allowed himself to get into this situation. He was not a cuddler. Yet there he was, his arm numb and asleep where it rested under Savannah's cheek. She had no problem staking her claim and getting comfortable in his bed, even if that meant using his various body parts as a pillow. Her favorites seemed to be his chest or shoulder. Though right now, his bicep was a close third.

He didn't want to move her, didn't want to rouse her from sleep. He'd promised her she'd be okay and found himself unable to break that promise in any form. If she needed to be close to another warm body while she slept, what hardship was it for him? Other than the awkward erection and numb arm—he'd live. She sighed contentedly and rolled in closer, throwing one leg over his hip which did nothing to help the blood flow racing south.

He knew if he crossed that physical boundary with Savannah he wouldn't be the gentle lover she deserved. The overwhelming feeling of want she stirred within him wouldn't allow for that. He'd fuck her hard and fast. And since he was pretty sure she was still a virgin, she deserved someone who would be careful, soft, and take his time. Another reason why he wasn't the man for the job. Cole shifted her knee to relieve the pressure of her warm thigh against his groin and tried to relax.

During times like this his mind often wandered and he couldn't help but remember the first time he'd laid eyes on her. She'd been a startled little thing, huddled in the corner, watching him with wide eyes. Even then she'd roused in him all kinds of protective instincts, made the alpha male inside him come out in a big way. And if his current cuddling status was any indication, she still did. He tightened his grip around her unconsciously drawing her nearer. Even if he couldn't act on the desire he felt for the woman in his bed, he sure as fuck wouldn't let anyone hurt her.

Savannah squirmed in her sleep, murmuring lightly. He brought his free hand to her hair, sweeping the tousled strands from her forehead to quiet her. She was too vulnerable, too damaged, which was exactly why he needed to stop thinking with his dick. Pronto.

Chapter 1

What a cluster fuck. Cole had seen some messed up things in his day, but the scene before him took the cake.

A stream of people fled through the front doors and others jumped from the first floor windows of the large grey compound. Then again, what had he expected when his squad gassed the place?

After waiting for the fumes to clear, and most of the bodies to filter out, he ran toward the building, rain pelting his jacket. He ducked through the door and removed his gas mask taking a tentative breath to test the air around him. There was only a slight tingle in his throat. It would do. He didn't plan on hanging out in the front area where the canister had crashed through the window anyway. His goal was to seek out the back rooms and find anyone still lingering inside. And bonus points if he found the cult's leader, Jacob, before his commander did. If Jacob was guilty of even half the crimes they had him on, Cole wouldn't mind punching the guy square in the jaw.

Jacob was a certified whackjob. He claimed to be a spiritual healer, and had about forty people swallowing his bullshit. When the FBI learned this morning of his plans to lead his followers in a suicide mission, they'd moved fast, warrant be damned. So far, it appeared they'd made it in time.

Cole adjusted the strap of his rifle and treaded along the hallway. He turned the corner, the lighting dim from the lack of windows, and listened for any sounds. Dead silence. Hearing nothing to indicate a threat, he entered the room on his right.

A young woman was huddled in the corner of the bedroom. She sat slumped against the wall, knees hugged to her chest. Her breath came in quick shallow gasps.

For a long second, Cole couldn't move, couldn't think. Something about this woman captivated his attention. Eyes, the color of emeralds, stared up at him in fear and confusion. Trembling hands hugged her legs tight to her chest. Unshed tears burned in that brilliant green gaze.

Snapping out of his daze, Cole stepped closer. The woman flinched and shrank back against the wall. She was shaking uncontrollably but her eyes followed his movements. He scanned the bedroom, checking for other victims or threats, but found only several bunk beds, clothes strewn across the floor, and a crib in the corner. Once the room was secure, Cole lowered his gun.

Procedure dictated he shout his command before taking action. But his gut told him a different tactic might be required.

'What's your name?' he asked, gazing down at her petite form.

'S-Savannah,' she stammered, her voice raspy.

He pulled in a deep lungful of air and crossed the room, his boots thudding against the tiled floor. She pressed back hard against the wall, watching him approach. He slung the rifle's strap over his shoulder, letting the weapon hang free and lifted his hands—palms out, fingers splayed—facing her. 'It's okay. I'm here to help.'

She watched him with wide eyes that held a flicker of curiosity. Though she remained hunkered down, she lifted her chin as he approached.

He considered helping her up, but he instinctively knew her hands would remain tightly locked in her lap.

He had two choices: pick her up and carry her out, or win over her trust. Trust took time. Making a split second decision, he crouched down and lifted her, securing one arm behind her knees, the other around her waist. A startled gasp escaped her throat, but as soon as Savannah was in his arms her body relaxed. She rested her head against his shoulder and let out a deep sigh, as if she'd been carrying around some great burden and was suddenly free now that she was in his arms. She laced her fingers behind his neck and buried her face in his chest, like it was the most natural thing in the world. Momentarily stunned by her warm body wrapped around his, it took him a moment to get his feet moving.

He carried her through the building, catching surprised glances from the other agents as he held her tightly to his chest, crossing through the emptying rooms. She sank into him, into his protection and that measure of complete trust and surrender twisted something inside Cole, invoking a feeling he'd never encountered until now.

'Found a girlfriend back there, Fletcher?' one of the guys said, followed by a wave of laughter.

Normally, he'd snap back a retort, but he couldn't focus on much with her locked in his embrace. The fragrant waves of dark hair spilling over her shoulders, the soft curves of her body molding to his hard chest was more than a little distracting.

When they entered the front room, Savannah finally spoke. 'You can set me down now.' Her breath was warm against his neck and it sent a tingling rush down his spine.

He lowered her feet to the floor, suddenly finding himself reluctant to let her go. She looked at him and blinked twice, her mouth opening to draw in a shuddering breath. He felt just as speechless. Emotions he'd thought long dead stirred within him.

She turned and strode toward the few people still left in the building—a small group of children lined up against the far wall, looking bewildered.

It was no big shocker that a group of male agents were clueless as to what to do with the littlest victims. At least they had enough sense to bring them inside out of the rain while they waited for the vans to arrive.

Savannah kneeled before the children and spoke to them in a hushed voice. Whatever she said had the power to calm them. Several of the older kids swiped at tears and fixed on brave faces. The littlest one, a toddler with blonde, curls crawled onto her lap.

At first Cole had been solely focused on the mission—to capture Jacob—but now he wondered what would happen to the women and children. Well, mainly the young woman, Savannah.

When the vans arrived, he watched her help the children fashion capes out of discarded blankets to shield them from the rain. Then she paraded them outside to the waiting vehicles.

The unfamiliar sting of worry pierced his chest. This was the only home they knew, and it was now the center of an FBI investigation. They'd been literally cast out into the cold. He shook the thought away. Damn. He must be going soft. This was the same kind of thing he'd counseled junior agents on—never get emotionally involved in a case. It was a mind fuck waiting to happen. But watching Savannah walk away, her shapely backside and legs encased in a pair of jeans, damp hair hanging down her back, he knew better than to pretend he wasn't affected. Damn it.

As Cole stood in the doorway, the cold air snatched his breath away instantly, forcing him to pull the edges of his jacket tighter. He couldn't help thinking about her lush, soft curves and how she'd felt in his arms. Wanting her was a powerful, primal need, an instinctive response, and one he hadn't experienced in a long time. The difference was he'd never act on it.

Hell, he was willing to bet he'd never even see her again. And that was for the best.

Chapter 2

Cole didn't count on the woman appearing in his dreams. For the past several nights, she'd played a starring role. Though each dream contained a different scenario, they were all a variation of the actual take-down. Only in his dreams he'd spoken to her, made her laugh. He'd calmed her worries, and eased that little line that creased her forehead. Then he'd leaned in close to inhale the scent of her hair, carried her to his SUV, and tucked her safely inside. He woke each morning cursing himself out. He didn't get to keep her. But damn if his subconscious knew it, uncooperative prick that it was.

Now in the office, sitting at his desk with the sunlight streaming through the cheap blinds, dotting his computer screen with flecks of light, Cole scrubbed a hand across his stubbly jaw. The case that had consumed much of his time over the past month had come to an unsatisfying conclusion. Jacob had been found dead in an out-building adjacent to the compound, of an apparent self-inflicted gunshot wound. From the Bureau's standpoint, the case was all but closed. But Cole had spent the last several days milling through the mountains of files they'd accumulated on the group, making sure everything was done correctly He kept finding himself stuck on details that might somehow relate to Savannah. Then he gave up trying to be sly, and read every single note they had on her. She was nineteen and had joined the group with her mother when she was just seven years old. Her mother, believed to have been one of Jacob's lovers, passed away when Savannah was fifteen. Savannah had been living with the group in the compound just outside of Dallas ever since. That God damn cult was all she'd ever known.

Cole knew that all of the children, fourteen of them under the age of eighteen, had been taken into Child Protective Services. He had no idea what would become of those of legal age. He supposed once they were brought in for questioning and their statements taken, many of them would be free to go.

Gulping weak coffee from a paper cup, it took him a moment to realize his boss was standing in front of his desk.

'You look like shit, Fletcher.'

Cole didn't bother explaining he hadn't been sleeping well, preferring not to get in a conversation about exactly why that was the mysterious girl he'd rescued from the compound still clouding his thoughts even in his sleep—knowing that excuse wouldn't go over well with Norman.

Cole rubbed a hand across the back of his neck. 'Thanks,' he muttered.

'You need a break, Cole. You've been working eighty-hour weeks nonstop the past few months. Now that this case is over, I'm not assigning you to another until you take some time off.'

'What are you talking about, a leave of absence?' Cole had heard of other guys messing up and getting forced into a leave, if only to make an example of them. But as far as he knew, he hadn't fucked anything up, at least not lately, and he was in line for a promotion at his next review cycle.

'No, like a vacation.' Norm's stern gaze met Cole's confused one. 'You've heard of a vacation, right?'

Cole almost laughed, and would have, had he not been pissed at where this conversation was headed. It was the exact same conversation he'd had with his meddling older sister, Marissa, just a few days before. When she'd stopped by last weekend and seen the dark circles under his eyes, she'd challenged him on when he'd last taken time off. The truth was he'd never purposefully taken time off work. He wouldn't know what to do with himself. The one and only time he'd taken some personal days was the standard bereavement leave when his parents were killed six years ago.

Norm was still staring down at him expectantly. 'I checked with HR, and they told me you've never taken a single vacation day in six years with the Bureau.'

No shit. And for good reason. He'd be bored as hell in two hours. 'And what exactly do you expect me to do?'

'How the hell should I know? Do whatever it is people do when they have time off work.'

'Thanks, but I'm actually good. Just give me another case, Norm.'

'This is non-negotiable.'

He wasn't averse to taking on Norm, but he wasn't stupid enough to argue with him when that vein in his forehead was throbbing.

Cole stood, knowing it'd be pointless to press the issue, and scooped up the files from his desk. He'd just work from home. Norm cracked a sideways grin and pulled the files from his hands.

'No. No bringing work home. Get a massage, go to the fucking Bahamas; I don't care what you do, as long as you take a break. Don't come back until Monday. *Next* Monday,' he clarified.

Fuck. A week off of work with nothing to do? He'd go insane. Unless…

No, he knew he shouldn't check up on Savannah, but once the idea had planted itself firmly in his mind, he knew it'd be damn near impossible to shake.

Cole spent the first two days of his vacation much like he spent every other weekend: catching up on sleep, hitting the gym, grabbing some takeout and parking it on the couch with a beer and flipping aimlessly through the TV channels.

But by the time Monday morning rolled around, he knew he was in over his head. There was no way he'd survive another week of this shit. He was already bored out of his mind, and it was day one of his Bureau-enforced vacation. Damn Norm.

Thoughts of Savannah continued to occupy his mind, and he found himself wondering where she was and if she was doing okay. After his third cup of coffee, he was jittery and pacing. Damn, he'd be crawling the walls of his condo by noon if he didn't get out and do something.

Cole made a snap decision, knowing he wouldn't be able to let the thoughts of Savannah go. Not until he knew she was okay. It was simple curiosity, nothing more. Plus, it'd give him something to do to occupy his time. A win all round. He'd do a simple stakeout, no big deal. After a quick phone call to another agent that morning, he had a good idea where they'd taken her.

The safe house.

She was taken to the only nearby facility with an opening— a transitional housing development on the shady side of town. Something about it didn't sit right with him. She was too innocent and good-looking to be somewhere like that.

He would stakeout the house, assuming she was still there. Since the file hadn't mentioned any other family, he was betting she was. Once he saw her with his own eyes, and confirmed she was safe and doing well, he would let it go.

Chapter 3

Fall was Savannah's favorite time of year. The brutal heat of the Texas summer had dissipated and left the air around her pleasantly warm, and more comfortable than stifling. She was taking her third walk of the day. With nothing to do other than sit and worry over the kids, she preferred to be outside, moving, rather than sitting in the grungy halfway house.

She rounded the corner of the block she'd grown familiar with over the past several days, surprised she hadn't worn a path into the sidewalk by now. There was a small park across the street. She considered stopping to watch the children playing, but kept going, knowing it would only dredge up memories that would make her cry.

She couldn't quite believe things had ended the way they did. She felt conflicted being away from the compound, empty in a weird way. It was all she knew, but she'd dreamed of leaving the overly strict compound for the last few years. She'd become disillusioned with their whole way of life after her mother passed away four years ago. But there were certain things, and people, she'd miss. She already missed the bustle of activity, always having someone to talk to. She thought of Dillon, the only other person her age, and wondered where he was.

When the sun began to sink lower in the sky, she resigned herself to spending another night at the house. She'd come to despise it for no other reason than how alone she felt there. She turned right at the corner, surprised that she didn't recognize her surroundings. She'd been so lost in thought, and over-confident in her ability to navigate, that she hadn't paid attention to where she'd wandered. She turned in a circle, searching out a landmark, or street sign she'd recognize; but unfortunately it did little good. She was lost.

She took a deep breath and willed herself to stay calm. But the façade lasted about two seconds. She had no one to call and didn't even know the address of the house. She was completely and utterly alone. After growing up in a household with a dozen different women mothering her, the realization was a stark one. She'd never been on her own. And she was already failing at it.

Savannah wiped away the tears that had begun to escape her eyes. What would she do if couldn't find the house again? The street had started with an L, hadn't it? She supposed she could go into a nearby shop and ask if they knew of a halfway house close by. She'd probably sound like a crazy person, but what other options did she have? She pulled in a deep breath, regaining some composure, and looked through the window of a convenience store. The guy at the counter met her eyes, then stared straight at her boobs. Nope. Not going in there. Gaze cast down, she kept walking.

With the thud of her shoes against the sidewalk and the pounding rhythm of her heart guiding her, Savannah continued on. The purr of a car engine lingered behind her. Not passing. Shoot. This wasn't a great part of town to be alone in. What had she been thinking? So she quickened her stride, but the car kept pace.

A large black SUV stopped alongside her. The dark tinted window lowered. A rush of panic washed over her, and tears sprang to her eyes.

'Savannah?'

The rough male voice knew her name. She stumbled to a halt and dared a glance in his direction. She was met with the concerned gaze of the FBI agent who had rescued her after the compound was raided. He was tall, and broad shouldered with dark hair, stubble dusting his jaw and his dark eyes were locked on hers. She ventured a step closer to his SUV. She didn't know his name, or what he intended, but something in his dark gaze gripped the very depths of her, and she knew instinctively that she could trust him. At least she hoped she could. He hadn't hurt her that night. His touch had been strong, but gentle. Summoning, her courage, she turned to face him.

Cole couldn't believe his luck, that he had quite literally spotted Savannah on the way to the safe house.

Her face was streaked with tears and her eyes wild. Shit, she looked scared. Had someone done something to her? The thought drove him nuts.

'Savannah?' he repeated.

Without waiting for her to respond, Cole slammed his gearshift into park and hopped out, crossing the front of the SUV to stand before her.

He lifted her chin, inspecting her face and neck for marks, and gripped her upper arms to turn her in a circle, looking her over completely. She appeared unharmed, so he didn't understand why she was crying. 'What happened?'

She swallowed and looked down at the sidewalk between their feet.

'Hey.' He brushed her hand with his. 'You remember me, right?'

She met his eyes and gave him a hesitant nod. 'What's your name?' she asked, a nervous hitch in her voice.

'Colby Fletcher.' He offered her his hand, and she slipped her delicate fingers into his palm.

'Colby,' she repeated in barely a whisper.

'You can call me Cole. Everyone else does. Or Fletcher, or Fletch. You know, whatever…'

She grinned, more with her eyes than her mouth. His babbling had apparently scored some points.

'Now tell me what's wrong,' he pushed. He didn't mean for it to come out as a command, but he needed to know what had happened to her, manners aside.

'I went for a walk and got lost,' she said simply.

Cole nearly sagged in relief. Thank fuck. That, he could fix. God, if something had happened to her, he didn't think he could've handled it. Not with the worry that'd been churning in his gut the last several days. 'Come on, I can drive you back.' He turned for the driver's side again, but Savannah remained rooted to the sidewalk. He returned to the spot where she stood and spoke to her in hushed tones. 'You can trust me, okay?'

Her eyes flashed to his. He'd forgotten how green they were. She squinted and blinked several times, as if she was deciding. It was cute. Without another word, Savannah opened the passenger door and climbed inside.

Cole's skin tingled, hyper-aware of just how close she was. She wore a pair of baggy jeans, torn at one knee and a long sleeved thermal tee, but the ill-fitting attire did nothing to temper the desire he felt. He gripped the steering wheel tighter, his hands itching to fold her body against his own. Shit, his libido was out of control when it came to this girl. Maybe he really did need a vacation. Somewhere with sand and lots of women in bikinis. Somewhere the hell away from Savannah.

Neither spoke during the short ride back to the halfway house. Cole stopped in front of the two-story, pale gray house flaking in paint. Both his and Savannah's attention was captured by a group of guys sitting on the wide front porch, arguing loudly.

Savannah fiddled nervously with the door handle, but made no move to exit the car.

'Listen, I don't have to take you back right away…we could grab a cup of coffee.'

Relief washed over her face. 'Yes.'

There was no way he was sending her back inside that house just yet.

Over steaming mugs of coffee at a nearby café, Cole attempted small talk, but mostly they sat in comfortable silence. Savannah seemed distracted and somber. He wondered if she was counting down the minutes until she had to go back to that house, and dreading it just as much as he was. 'Do you have any family you can stay with?' he asked finally.

A deep searing gaze communicated her need. Cole's worst assumptions were proven correct — she was all alone. She swallowed and shook her head. 'My mom passed away when I was fifteen, and I never met my father. I suppose I could find one of the women from Jacob's group, but I don't know…'

'Are you hungry? Have you eaten? We could get you something.' Cole couldn't stop himself from peppering her with questions.

She kept her gaze cast down and shook her head. 'I'm fine.' Savannah sat quietly in her seat, her thin fingers wound tightly around the coffee mug.

Cole wished there was something more he could do for her. He wasn't sure what to say, how to help, so he sat silently across from her sipping his coffee.

By the time they reached the house again, darkness had blanketed the sky. Cole shifted into park, turning off the engine. 'I'll walk you inside.'

The house itself was large, but poorly maintained. The furniture was old and unmatched, the beige carpet stained and threadbare. Cole didn't see much of the first floor, beyond a dingy living room, before she led him upstairs. There were several closed doors along the long hallway. Savannah stopped at the second door on the right. The key fumbled between her fingers, clanking against the wooden door. After three failed attempts to unlock it, Cole removed it from her trembling hand, and deftly opened the door.

The first thing he noticed was the odor—the room smelled like wet gym socks. Savannah flipped on the light and took several steps into the room. A single narrow cot on the floor and a chair in the corner containing stray articles of clothing were the only furnishings.

Fuck. He couldn't just leave her here, could he?

Savannah stepped in closer, wrapping her arms around his waist and tucking her head under his chin. 'Thank you,' she whispered.

Her eagerness at physical contact surprised him, but he only hesitated a moment before wrapping his arms around her. Cole patted her back, hating that his attempts at soothing her were clumsy and awkward. He'd never been good at this kind of thing: emotions, touchy-feely crap. Maybe his presence would be enough to calm her. And although he didn't know how to show it, he felt protective. He wouldn't let anyone hurt her. If anyone so much as looked at her the wrong way, Cole would knock them on their ass. He held her for several long minutes until the beating of her heart slowed to normal, and she backed out of his arms.

Their eyes flashed to one another's at the sounds of an argument going on in the next room. Angry voices carried through the thin walls. Another argument. Cole and Savannah exchanged glances.

'Are you sure you'll be okay?'

She nodded, looking solemn.

'Here's my card.' He fished the card from his wallet and placed it in her trembling hand. 'Call me if you need anything.'

Savannah remained silent, glancing at the card, running her thumb along the raised lettering.

'Lock your door when I leave, okay?'

She nodded tightly, sucking her bottom lip into her mouth, as if there was something more she wanted to say, but stopped herself.

Cole left reluctantly He knew it was getting late, and as much as it pained him to leave her, he couldn't put it off any longer. He was sure he was crossing some sort of professional line even being here. He waited outside the door until he heard the lock slide into place, the sound not nearly as reassuring as he would have hoped.

Once he was outside, Cole took a deep breath and scrubbed his hands across his face. The cooling blast of autumn air filled his lungs, but did nothing to return him to his senses. He climbed inside his truck and gripped the steering wheel until his knuckles were white, trying to will himself to start the engine and drive away from her.

The lock on her door did little to calm her nerves. The deep, raspy voices of her male neighbors sent shivers down her spine. She huddled in closer to the thin, scratchy blanket.

The unfamiliar sounds and smells of the house left her on edge and shaking. The brief interlude with Cole had helped, but now that she was back in the bleak reality of the tiny room again, an impending panic attack throbbed in her chest.

Growing up the way she had, listening to Jacob's crazy rants about sex being dirty and diseased, and men of the world being fueled by only their lust, made her hyper-aware of the sounds in the rooms next to her. Their loud voices, crude glances, and grubby hands. Jacob constantly drilled into her that men would only want her for one thing.

Realization struck. She was alone. Totally and completely alone. Panic crept in to the edges of her brain, but she fought it, holding the darkness at bay. Just barely. *Think Savannah*. If she could go on after losing her mom, she could survive this, too. Didn't have much choice.

17

Her muscles trembled with the effort of lying still against the hard cot. She curled into a ball, hugging her knees to her chest, hoping it would sooth her. A loud whack against the wall made her jump. Savannah sat up in bed as the pain in her chest built. She drew a slow shaky breath and said a silent prayer. She tried not to break down again, but before she knew it, hot tears were freely streaming down her cheeks and she was wishing that Cole hadn't left. The only times she'd felt safe during the past week of this ordeal was when he was near.

She grabbed his card from the window sill and clutched it, crushing it to her heart. She wished she was stronger, that she didn't break down so easily. But after another loud thump against the wall, she let out a whimper and clamored under the blankets. She glanced at the door knob, the deadbolt still vertical, needing reassurance that the door was still locked.

She didn't want to leave the safety of her bedroom—and wouldn't have—had it not been for her insistent bladder urging her on. There were two bathrooms on the second floor, one was for women, the other for men. She'd come to learn over the past few days, tenants used whichever was closest, and since she had the bad fortune of being surrounded on both sides by male tenants, she knew the so-called ladies room was filthy and reeked of urine. The other bathroom was probably no better.

Still clutching Cole's card, Savannah cracked open the door and peeked both ways before tiptoeing towards the bathroom.

She made sure the toilet seat was clean before she relieved herself. As she stood washing her hands in the sink, she startled at the pale haunted-looking girl watching her from the mirror before realizing it was her own reflection.

The bulb above her flickered then died. Darkness made her head swim. She sucked in a deep breath and held it as her hands fumbled blindly in front of her, searching out the door. She'd hated the dark. Always had. Her hands still flailing in front of her, she begged herself not to panic.

Savannah swayed on her feet, blinking wildly against the darkness. Before she knew what was happening, she crashed against the wall, and felt a sharp blow ache through the back of her skull as she collapsed to the ground.

Chapter 4

Cole pulled into his underground parking garage just as the storm lit up the sky. An angry crack of lightning pierced the night, followed by a low rumble of thunder. It had been steadily raining his entire drive home, but the storm seemed to double its force within a matter of seconds, sheets of water pouring from the sky.

He was maneuvering into his assigned parking space when the call came in. His phone had been eerily silent all weekend, not even Marissa had been in touch. And at this late hour on Sunday, he didn't know who it could be. Fishing the phone from his center console, he noted the Dallas area code, but didn't recognize the number.

He couldn't understand her at first, her voice was high with tension, and barely above a whisper, but he soon realized it was Savannah. And she was asking him to come back. He pulled a u-turn and gunned the engine before her words even registered.

Keeping her on the line as he drove, he wanted to bombard her with questions, to find out if something had happened, but he resisted. Even as all that flashed through his mind, he'd found himself calming her, saying he would be right there, and flooring the gas pedal to get back to her. After ending the call, he slammed a fist against the dash. Damn, he shouldn't have left her at that place. But what choice did he have?

He thumbed the steering wheel, waiting for the light to change. He had to get her out of that house; probably check her into a hotel for the night. That would be the right thing to do, yet he knew with absolute certainty what he really wanted to do. He wanted to bring her home with him, where he could have her under the same roof and ensure she was safe.

When Cole arrived, he pressed the buzzer at the front door for the after-hours entrance. He was greeted by an older man, the night guard, he presumed.

'Where's Savannah?' He stormed past the man, following the sounds of soft sobs toward the back of the house. Entering an office, he found an older woman seated behind a desk, and Savannah crumpled in a ball on the chair across from her. 'Savannah,' his voice rasped.

She looked up and Cole nearly staggered a step back. Christ. It looked like someone had used her face as a punching bag. Her swollen and busted lip was encrusted with blood and her left eye was already darkening with a bruise. When she met his eyes she let out a soft sigh, seemingly comforted by his presence.

'Shh. I'm here.' He weaved his fingers under her hair to cradle the back of her neck. Then he turned his attention to the woman behind the desk. 'What the hell happened here?'

'Have a seat, Mr.....?'

'Cole Fletcher.' He took the chair next to Savannah.

She crawled into his lap, burying her face in his neck as little sobs racked her chest. His arms, working of their own accord, wound themselves around Savannah and shifted her to a more comfortable position on his lap.

Once Savannah was settled, his training kicked in and he began firing questions at the facility coordinator. She explained they'd briefly lost power in the storm, and when they went upstairs to check and make sure everyone was secure, they found Savannah unconscious on the bathroom floor, where she'd apparently fainted and smacked her head on the porcelain sink on her way down. His fingers automatically threaded into her hair, smoothing the bump he found on the back of her head.

The coordinator seemed unconcerned, like she'd dealt with these situations too many times. But he hadn't, and neither had Savannah. Vacant eyes stared at the wall across from him. He was worried that shock was beginning to set in. He soothed a hand up and down her back, not quite sure what to do to comfort her.

The woman behind the desk looked over the top of her glasses, mouth twisted into a disapproving frown. Cole could tell the woman was wondering exactly what kind of relationship he shared with Savannah.

His tone and questions were professional, yet Savannah's body currently wrapped around his said it was something else entirely. He chose not to identify himself as an agent, and let the woman think what she wanted.

Once in situated in his lap, Savannah's breathing returned to normal, and the steady thump of her heartbeat against his chest told him she was recovering. She was alright. Thank fucking God. He didn't understand why his presence calmed her – not like he had a lot to offer – but he wasn't about to question it. Not when she was so fragile.

The woman held up a hand. 'Listen, I know this isn't the Ritz, but if she wants to stay here, she can. If she wants to leave, fine. It's up to her.'

Savannah lifted her head from his chest and met Cole's eyes. 'Can you take me away from here?'

She couldn't understand what she was asking for. Of course Cole wanted to take her far away from this place, from the first time he'd laid eyes on the rundown house. But protocol and not crossing professional boundaries stirred in the back of his head.

He resisted the urge to smooth the tangled strands of hair from her face, but kept his arms locked around her middle. Savannah's bloodied lip, swollen face, and the exhaustion he could read on her features told him now might not be the time to argue. 'Okay. We can go.'

Tomorrow they'd figure everything out.

He lifted Savannah from the chair and held her like he had at the compound. And just as strong as before, the need to protect her flared up inside of him.

Carrying her out into the night, Cole opened the passenger door and helped her inside. He reached across her to buckle her seat belt. When his hands brushed her ribs, she startled, sucking in a shaky breath. He should probably check her over for injuries, assuming that she'd likely sustained some bumps and bruises, but his first priority was getting her out of here.

She was silent on the drive to his condo, not even asking where they were going. She implicitly trusted him. The feeling was heady.

He kept the radio low, he left Savannah to her thoughts, looking out the window as he drove. He snuck glances her way, wondering what she could possibly be thinking about. The awkward silence dug into his brain like a dripping faucet.

'This your first time in the city?' he asked.

Savannah kept her eyes on the passing buildings. 'We didn't leave the compound much.'

Of course. Stupid question. He tried again. 'Does your head hurt? How about your ribs?'

She ran her fingers through her matted hair, checking the bump. 'I think it's okay now.'

At least she'd stopped crying. Nothing made him panic more than a woman crying.

When he parked in his assigned parking space and turned off the engine, a hushed silence fell over them in the confined space.

His heart rate ramped up in sudden awareness of her. The light, feminine scent that clung to her skin, her petite frame, and the overwhelming desire to protect her— he couldn't deny the possessive ache that raced through his system.

'Why did you pass out, Savannah?'

She swallowed heavily. 'That place scared me. There were too many people…too many strange men…'

He nodded. It wasn't lost on him that he was a strange man to her, yet here she was alone with him too. 'This is where I live,' he said finally.

Her eyes widened. 'You brought me home with you?'

'Is that okay?'

She studied him, her expression weary and unsure and squirmed in her seat.

'I'm sorry; I didn't know where else to take you. Come inside, and if you decide not to stay, I'll take you anywhere you want to go.'

Seemingly satisfied, she climbed from the car.

Chapter 5

Savannah insisted she could walk, but Cole secured an arm around her waist and helped her inside. He tossed his keys onto the breakfast bar, retaining his hold on her.

He knew he shouldn't keep her here. God, Norm and the guys would have a fucking field day with this one. Sure, he brought his work home most nights, but this was a hell of a lot different. She could sleep in his guest room tonight, and then he'd have to take her to another safe house in the morning. For now, he just wanted her to feel safe. If he needed to install a bigger lock on her bedroom door to help her feel safe, so be it. They could pick up some pepper spray too.

Cole took a deep breath, trying to calm his nerves. The panic in her voice when she called had him wondering what exactly had happened once he left, but he didn't want to push her. He had a good enough idea from the facility coordinator. She'd likely panicked at the thought of being alone. If the living conditions of the compound were any indication, she'd grown up surrounded by people at all times. He had half a mind to tuck Savannah safely into his bed and forget protocol.

Her eyes darted around his condo, seeming to take in her surroundings. 'Come on.' He guided her down the hall. 'Let's get you cleaned up.'

He passed by the guest bath, knowing it wasn't stocked with what he needed. At his bedroom door, she paused briefly, her feet stopping at the threshold, her eyes trained on the massive bed. 'It's okay,' he urged. 'We're just going into the master bath.'

Her eyes drifted to the open door across the room, and she gave a nod, allowing him to urge her forward. The muscles in her face tensed, but her feet started moving again.

He flipped on the light, and cursed his lack of cleanliness. Various bottles and jars littered the counter — shaving cream, aftershave, deodorant, toothpaste — everything within his grasp since he got ready for work on autopilot. He cleared a spot on the counter by sweeping everything into a drawer and then lifted Savannah onto the counter in front of him.

He wet a washcloth and carefully washed her face, wiping away the traces of dried blood. Her breasts rose and fell with each shallow breath, and her wide green eyes watched his every move. They were inquisitive and bright with determination. He found himself drawn to her, wanting to discover all he could about the mysterious, beautiful girl who had grown up in a cult. She rubbed her hands up and down her arms in an effort to calm herself and regain some control over the situation. He could sense the desperation she felt, her outlook suddenly seeming quite bleak. He struggled to find words to soothe her, to reassure her, but came up short and instead just silently treated her injuries as best he could.

Once she was clean, he dabbed the cut above her eye with a cotton swab covered in ointment.

'How do you know how to do this?' she asked.

His eyes flicked to hers. They were so close that he could lean in and kiss her. 'Hmm? Oh, I've certainly been knocked around before. It's no big deal. You'll be good as new in a few days.'

She frowned. 'Knocked around? Because your job is dangerous?'

He recapped the ointment and considered her question. 'Yes, sometimes. Other times not. But actually I was thinking about my teen years. I was a bit of a trouble maker. My parents sent me to military school my last two years of high school.'

'Oh.' Her eyes were big and inquisitive, as if she wanted to ask more, but instead she looked down at her hands. 'How old are you now?'

'Twenty-seven,' he answered. *Too old for you.*

His eyes caught their reflection in the mirror and the serious expression in his features distracted him. His brow was knotted in concentration, and his mouth a tight line. He did his best to relax the tense set of his shoulders, knowing he needed to be calm if he wanted Savannah to relax too.

A few heartbeats later she visibly relaxed, her breathing smoothing out, and her hands uncurling in her lap. Her features were entirely feminine, from her long dark hair that curled at the ends, to her almond-shaped eyes fringed in dark lashes, to her smooth, soft skin. Savannah was a natural beauty.

Catching his own reflection in the mirror, Cole, in contrast, was all male. His jaw was shadowed in dark stubble and his body lean and sculpted with muscle, which he worked hard to maintain. Compared to Savannah, he was hard plains and jagged edges, all except for his full sensuous mouth. More than one ex-girlfriend had complimented his lips, and what he could do with his mouth. When he was with a woman, he used every weapon in his seduction arsenal — his mouth, tongue, hands, even his strength—often liking the feel of power, the crude masculinity of picking up a woman and holding her weight as he fucked her. It had been several months though since he'd taken a lover, and his body was growing restless with pent-up desire.

Once Savannah was cleaned up, Cole stepped back and met her eyes. They were still swimming with tears and her breathing was little more than shallow gasps for air. He could tell that the slightest thing would set her off again. Shit. So much for relaxing.

Savannah was an absolute mess. To be expected. She'd probably been through hell and back these past several days, and getting bruised up earlier had sent her over the edge. A girl like Savannah, who'd grown up so sheltered with such a strange upbringing, had no defenses to protect herself from the pure chaos this world dished up. He knew from the FBI files that the women and children were rarely seen outside the compound.

Cole, on the other hand, was hardened, bitter, and certainly not delusional enough to believe in happily-ever-after. He'd seen too much working for the Bureau the past six years, and experienced pain firsthand when his parents were hit and killed by a meth addict who was drunk and high at the time of the accident. Still, he felt for Savannah, felt sorry for her in a way. She wasn't the type to fare well on her own, that was obvious.

He lifted her chin and rubbed a slow circle against her jaw. 'I've got you. It's going to okay.'

She gave a heavy nod and somber eyes met his. 'So what happens now?'

Cole could read the apprehension on her face. The honest truth was, he didn't know what happened next, but he knew one thing was certain; he wasn't taking her back to that house. They both needed some sleep, and they would figure the rest out later. 'Now we sleep. Come on, I'll show you around.'

He helped her from the counter, and led her through the condo, giving her a brief tour. He guided Savannah to the living room and encouraged her to sit on the sofa. He was about to turn and head for the kitchen to get her some water and pain reliever, but she silently took his hand and held it in her own, her eyes pleading with him to stay.

He sat down beside her and she wordlessly lowered her head to rest against his thigh, nestling herself into him. Cole couldn't breathe, couldn't think. He dared not move with her head resting on his denim clad thigh. She bent her legs up onto the couch beside her, curling into the fetal position, and closed her eyes. He didn't know what to do with his hands and settled for fisting one beside him, and placed the other carefully on Savannah's shoulder. He let her sleep, unwilling to rustle her from the spot she'd claimed.

When he woke a short time later, it took him a moment to realize who the warm body pressed against him belonged to. Savannah. He lifted his head and surveyed his body, and in turn hers. They had shifted in sleep so that he was stretched out on his back, and she was lying half on him, and half on the couch. Savannah woke when he moved and their eyes flicked to each other's. He mumbled an apology and disentangled himself from her grip.

He scrubbed a hand across his jaw. He'd never felt so out of place in his own house. The rumble of Savannah's stomach made him smile and broke some of the tension. She clapped a hand over her belly. 'Are you hungry?' He chuckled.

'Yes.' She nodded.

'Come on. Let's see what we can rustle up in the kitchen.' He led her into the large kitchen at the front of his condo. 'I have to warn you though, I don't cook.'

'I do.' Her hand on his forearm stopped him, and she motioned for him to take a seat at a stool tucked under the kitchen island. 'Let me.'

'Are you sure you're up for that?' Cole questioned.

'It'll help me feel better, more normal. I used to cook all the time at the compound.'

Cole relented, sinking onto the seat. The time blinked at him from the clock on the microwave. It was three in the morning. He suddenly found himself thankful that he didn't have to go to work in a few hours, though given the hour, he wasn't as tired as he expected. He watched Savannah move about his kitchen, surveying the sad contents of his fridge, removing items from the pantry and cabinets as she went.

'Sorry I don't have much.'

'You have eggs,' she said, placing the carton on the counter.

He frowned, not able to recall the last time he went grocery shopping. 'You might want to check the expiration date on those.'

She lifted the carton to read the date printed on the bottom. 'Hmm. We don't have eggs.' She pulled a box from the pantry. 'Pasta then.'

It didn't escape his notice that she'd said *we*, implying it was the two of them together against all the bullshit they'd suffered so far. He didn't know what to make of that, but nodded. 'Fine.' She was holding up surprisingly well, given the craziness of the situation.

She dumped an entire package of penne pasta into a pot of boiling, salted water. Cole watched her movements, and decided he liked having her in his kitchen. A satisfied little smile tugged at her lips, and she moved about effortlessly.

Only once they were seated in the small breakfast nook, nibbling on pasta with a rich sauce she made from milk, butter and parmesan cheese, did he venture to ask about her past.

'Can I ask you a few questions about the compound…and how you grew up?' He knew some of the details from reading the files on the case, but he wanted to hear the story in Savannah's own words.

She nodded reluctantly. Her eyes were skittish—looking anywhere but at him.

'You just let me know if there's anything you're not comfortable answering. And we won't talk about it.' He didn't intend to push her too far tonight. She'd been through enough, but he figured if she was going to be staying in his home, there was some basic information he'd need to know, if only to make sure she felt as comfortable as possible.

'What was it like growing up there?'

She took a deep breath and began reiterating some of what he'd read in the case files. Jacob wanted to create a perfect community:

they grew their own food, sold goods at farmer's markets, and were entirely self-contained. He taught them that the outside world was a dangerous place, and that people were dirty and couldn't be trusted. He taught them that germs and diseases spread from sexual contact would eventually kill off most of the population and they wouldn't be able to procreate, so Jacob's followers needed to separate themselves to live cleanly.

'How did your mother get involved?' Cole asked.

Savannah folded her hands in her lap. 'She fell for him. He was a charmer, a smoother talker, confident. Easily able to convince people to follow him.'

Cole knew that much from the information the Bureau had collected in the file.

'He could be very persuasive. When he spoke, people listened,' Savannah explained.

'What about you; did you believe his teachings?'

She nodded. 'At first. I didn't know any different. But as I got older, I began to wonder. I had this urge to see for myself; it nagged at me sometimes.'

Finding her plate empty, Cole served up another helping of pasta for Savannah before urging her to continue.

She stabbed a forkful of noodles, looking lost in thought. 'Most of all, I just wanted to go to school. Jacob couldn't understand it. He tried to convince me it wasn't safe. Boys out there…' she stopped suddenly, her eyes dropping to her plate.

'What? You can tell me.'

'He said the boys would only want one thing from me — to get in my panties.'

Had anyone been in her panties? And why did that thought make him want to punch someone? He had no right — no claim to her — yet he couldn't help the possessive streak that surged inside him. 'Okay. So I take it you didn't go to school?'

'No. But I refused to relent and finally convinced Jacob to hire a tutor for me, so I could get my high school diploma. We met at the local library twice a week for the last year. I was one of the few given permission to leave the compound.'

Wow. He'd been right about her determination.

They ate in silence for several minutes. Cole didn't want to push her too fast, he was happy that she was comfortable talking to him at all.

'This is delicious, by the way.' He stabbed a forkful of pasta and managed another bite, though he was stuffed four bites ago. He had a healthy appetite, but Savannah had made enough to feed an army — if the still full platter of pasta on the table between them was any indication.

'You obviously know a lot about me,' Savanna said, twirling a strand of long hair around her finger. 'But if I'm going to stay here, shouldn't I know more about you?'

He shrugged. 'What do you want to know?'

She thought about it for a moment, continuing to play with her hair. Cole's attention was pulled from her brilliant green eyes to her mouth and the way she absently toyed with stray lock of hair.

'No wife? No girlfriend?'

'It's just me.'

'How come?'

He thought about how to respond, not about why — he didn't want the responsibility, the heartache that came with loss of a loved one ever again. But he took his time, considering which answer to give her. 'It's the way I like it.'

Savannah frowned slightly. 'Doesn't that get lonely? What about your family? Are they nearby?'

Cole remained quiet, watching the way her hand stilled its movements when she grew unsure of herself, wondering if she'd overstepped a boundary with that question.

'That's another thing you and I have in common.'

Her eyes searched his, trying to understand. 'Your parents…'

'They're gone. Have been for a few years now. It's just my sister Marissa and me. She's three years older and a pain in the ass,' he added, hoping to add some levity back into the moment which had suddenly grown heavier than he'd bargained for.

'I'm sorry,' she whispered, her eyes never wavering from his.

Realization sparked between them and their gazes remained locked together. Her eyes softened and prodded his dark stare until they were no longer strangers, but two people connecting from a shared loss that wounded so deeply, it never quite healed.

He took a slow, shaky breath. This wasn't part of the deal. He couldn't be getting soft now. Just because he'd brought his work home, so to speak, didn't mean it was okay for him to get all mushy. Christ, what came next? Crying on each other's shoulders? Knitting a God damn blanket. No fucking way. He'd do what he had to do to help Savannah. He wasn't okay with seeing a woman suffer. That was all this was. He would not get emotionally involved. Couldn't. Not again. He had a cabinet full of prescription meds that were the result of him getting involved in something he shouldn't have once before.

'Thanks,' he bit out, more than ready to change the topic.

The remnants of food between them had grown cold, and Savannah looked positively exhausted. She sat slumped in her chair, her head leaning in her hand.

'Come on, let's get you to bed.' He placed their dishes in the sink and guided Savannah to the guest room.

Cole's home wasn't what Savannah had expected. She wasn't quite sure what she'd been expecting, but the large, modern third-floor loft with floor to ceiling windows and furniture with sleek, clean lines was unanticipated. She was too exhausted to explore, being overtired and fighting off a panic attack would do that to you, but she dutifully followed behind Cole, trying her best to listen as he pointed out things out to her. The small breakfast nook opened to a large living room with an espresso colored sectional sofa facing a large flat screen TV.

She'd already grown to love the large spotless kitchen, with its stainless steel appliances and rustic butcher-block island, even if the sight of it initially caused a pang of sadness to hit her chest. Thinking of cooking made her think of the compound, which made her think of the children. She worried about where they were now, and if they were being well cared for. Especially little Britta. The five year old girl was so smart and so tough, the toughest little girl she knew, and yet she looked so sad when she was loaded into the van with the other children. She hoped Britta was okay. Wished she could find her… But she'd put that out of her mind as she had worked, whipping up a basic recipe for fettuccine alfredo. She couldn't say she'd ever made that particular dish at three in the morning, but her options had been limited with such a poorly stocked kitchen.

She found herself wondering who took care of Cole, and thought it unusual that he wasn't married. He was in his late-twenties, he was kind and attractive. But just as quickly as the thoughts had entered her head, she'd pushed them away. She had no business wondering about his love life.

She followed Cole down the hallway, where he pointed out a large marble-floored guest bathroom and his bedroom, which she'd already seen, before stopping at another door just across from his.

He cleared his throat. 'This is the guest room.' He gestured for her to enter.

She stepped around him, entering the spacious room deco-rated in creams and whites. The large inviting bed in the center of the room drew her forward. When she pressed a hand into the center of the plush bed, there was no way she'd willing go back to sleeping on that hard, stained cot. The bed was outfitted in the softest blankets she'd ever felt. She toured the room, running her hand along the smooth curves of the dark wood dresser and then turned to face Cole. She wondered if she'd be allowed to stay. There was something about him — she sensed it from the first time she saw him at the compound. Though she probably should have feared him, she felt comforted by his presence.

'You can, ah, sleep here.' He rubbed a hand along the back of this neck. His bicep flexed, pulling against the T-shirt he wore. He had large, powerful muscles in his back, shoulders and arms, but somehow Savannah knew he wouldn't hurt her. He didn't strike her as the violent type.

'Thank you,' she murmured. She tried to imagine herself living in a place so nice, but it was too big and too empty to feel comfortable. She was accustomed to sleeping in a bunk room with other women and children, relaxing to the sounds of breathing or soft snores. But still, she appreciated his providing this room, where at least she would be safe. She'd already noted the door had its own lock.

They stood facing each other, neither speaking, but each studying the other. Savannah shifted her weight, looking down at her baggy jeans and sweatshirt. She didn't have a change of clothes, let alone pajamas or a toothbrush, but she wasn't about to ask Cole for anything else. He'd been too kind already, and she didn't want to wear out her welcome or cause him any objections to her staying.

Savannah was still standing in the center of the guest room, her bare feet buried in the plush carpeting. Cole suddenly found himself grateful for his sister Marissa's interior decorating help. He'd resisted it at first, but she'd slowly worn him down, reminding him that he might still be a bachelor, but he wasn't twenty-two anymore, and he was making good money. She said it was time to live like a grown-up. So he'd gotten a new bedroom set for himself, or more accurately he went along with Marissa to the furniture store, and handed over his credit card once she'd picked everything out.

She'd redecorated his place room by room, finishing with the guest room Savannah now stood in. He'd told Marissa it was a waste of money. This room had never held a guest in his three years of living here; it was where he kept his seldom used ironing board, luggage set and mountain bike. But now watching Savannah walk towards the bed and press her palm into the center of the fluffy comforter, he silently praised Marissa's intervention, not that he'd ever admit that to her.

'Wait right here. I'll be back.' Cole returned a moment later with a pair of his sweat pants and an old T-shirt, handing them to Savannah. 'You can wear this if it helps.'

Savannah accepted the clothes gratefully, and Cole left the room so she could change. A few minutes later, he tapped on the door with his knuckles. 'Are you decent?'

She opened the door and stood before him. The baggy clothes seemed to swallow her.

'We'll figure everything out in the morning. Just get some rest, okay?'

Savannah nodded, yawning sleepily. Cole watched her crawl into the bed, his chest tightening at the sight of her in his clothes, looking so small and helpless in the big bed. 'Night,' he uttered, his voice surprisingly tight.

He was grateful he had a few days off to help Savannah figure things out. How he would use those days, he had no idea. Of course, he would have to go back to work soon, and he had his Sunday visits with Abbie—which he hoped Savannah didn't need to know about. But one thing at a time. She was safe and warm in the guest bedroom, and that was good enough for now.

Chapter 6

When Cole woke the following morning, or afternoon as it were, it took him a moment to place the sounds coming from inside his apartment. *Savannah*. His heart did a little happy dance in his chest at the thought of finding her in his kitchen. He stretched and went to investigate. When he entered the kitchen, his bare feet thudding against the wood floor, Savannah looked up and froze like she'd been caught doing something wrong.

'Hi,' he offered, attempting to reassure her.

Her features softened. 'Hi.'

Cole scanned the mixing bowls and ingredients spread across his counters, and the island covered in a dusting of flour. 'Did you sleep okay?'

Savannah's eyes wandered the length of Cole's bare chest and stopped at the trail of fine hair grazing his lower stomach and disappearing under his waistband. She cleared her throat and looked down at her hands. 'Mmm hmm,' she stammered.

Cole bit his lip to keep from chuckling. His muscular physique always got positive reviews from the opposite sex. And he was surprised to see that even after all Savannah had been through, she still noticed him. He worked hard to keep in top physical shape, kick-boxing three times a week, lifting weights, and running the rest of the days. He glanced down at his naked chest and abs. His pants had slipped ever so slightly down on his hips, exposing his lower abdominals and the lines along his sides that formed a deep V at his hips. He tightened the drawstring, doubling the knot. *Down boy.* Now was not the time to get a hard on.

He rarely wore anything to bed but had tugged on a pair of pajama pants last night just in case Savannah needed anything in the middle of the night. That way he wouldn't have to fumble for his clothes in the darkness, or risk terrifying the poor girl with his naked manhood. He hadn't bothered with a shirt; he found the material too damn restrictive. He preferred the feel of his satin sheets against his bare skin — it was the one comfort he allowed himself.

'I'm making pancakes. I hope that's okay,' Savannah said quietly.

A box of mix sat on the counter. 'Of course that's okay. Thank you.' Cole crossed the kitchen to start a pot of coffee, stepping around her and noticing how unaccustomed he was to having someone in his space, though it wasn't entirely unwelcome.

'Sorry, I didn't know how to operate that thing.' Savannah eyed the coffee maker like it had personally offended her.

'Come here, I'll show you.'

Once Savannah had wiped her hands on a dish towel and sidled up next to Cole, he couldn't resist guiding her in between himself and the counter, so she was closer to the coffee maker, he told himself.

Savannah sucked in a breath at the contact, but didn't protest, allowing him to maneuver her body as he pleased. He demonstrated how to add fresh beans to the grinder and then how to set the beans to roast, then brew. The coffee maker was fussier than he was used to, but it had been a gift from Marissa last Christmas, and now he was addicted to fresh roasted coffee beans.

Neither of them moved away as the coffee began to drip into the waiting carafe. A sudden vision of lifting her hair off the back of her neck and leaning in to plant a kiss on her soft skin danced through his mind. He was just inches from pressing into her, grinding his hips into her ass. He felt his cock stir and knew their lesson was over.

'Let's eat,' he grumbled.

Savannah stood in stunned silence as he stalked from the kitchen. He grabbed a T-shirt and threw it on before sitting down at the breakfast bar. Savannah slid a stack of pancakes in front of him.

'Thanks.' He cast a quick glance up at her. He didn't realize having this beautiful young woman in his home would affect him like this. He was a professional. He shouldn't be affected by her.

He watched her move through the apartment, bending at the waist to collect the pile of mail he'd left by his arm chair, shuffling into the kitchen to arrange it on the counter and biting her lip as she studied a spot on the counter before wiping it away. Her lips were full and pink and he found himself wondering what they'd taste like before quickly pushing the thought away.

As she stood at the kitchen counter, Cole appraised her profile. Small but perky chest, dark hair curling around her shoulders, a flat stomach, and a nice shapely ass. He appreciated a fine ripe ass and getting that rounded backside in his palms played through his mind like a song on repeat, no matter how many times he reminded himself it wasn't happening.

The tiny cut on her lower lip had healed quickly, just the faintest line of pink visible if you were looking for it. Savannah looked up and met his eyes, her mouth dropping open in an unspoken question.

He needed to stop staring at her mouth or she was going to get the wrong idea. He didn't bring her here for any sinister purpose. He wasn't expecting anything in return for letting her stay.

He found his voice. 'Come sit down and eat with me.'

Savannah obeyed, carrying an extra plate and set of silverware over the breakfast bar to join him.

She helped herself to a few pancakes from the platter stacked high between them. Cole was glad to see that she didn't seem overly self-conscious or shy.

She cut her pancakes into little pieces but still hadn't taken a bite.

'How are you doing this morning?' he asked, trying his best at playing a nurturing role, something new for him.

She swallowed heavily and gazed over at him. 'Is it stupid that I miss it there?'

The compound? He supposed it was all she knew. 'No, I guess not. They were the only family you had.'

She nodded. 'There are some things I won't miss.'

He left her alone to her thoughts, fighting the urge to push her for details. He appreciated her personality — she didn't feel the need to fill the silence with pointless chatter. She was more observer of the world than outright contributor, and he could relate. He approached most things with a healthy dose of suspicion, and relationships for him were no different. They were each still feeling each other out, each on guard, but for likely different reasons. She was a vulnerable shell-shocked girl in a stranger's home, and he was a hardened FBI agent who'd experienced more than his fair share of loss. He rubbed a hand along the back of his neck. Christ, what a pair.

After a few seconds of quietly picking at her thumbnail, she asked, 'Do you think anyone from the compound could find me here?'

He doubted that'd be possible. She was supposed to be at the halfway house. Though if someone was interested enough and started poking around, the facility coordinator may remember Cole and she could be tracked down through him, but why would anyone bother?

'Why are you asking?'

'There was someone…'

'Someone what?'

She looked down, once again becoming fascinated with her thumbnail.

'Answer me.' He didn't intend the brute force behind his voice.

'Jacob's son.'

Cole racked his brain. The file mentioned that Jacob had a twenty-one year old son, Dillon, but he hadn't been living at the compound at the time of the raid. 'Dillon.'

She nodded.

'Is he dangerous?'

'No, nothing like that.' She hesitated for a beat, but before Cole could probe again, she released a sigh and continued. Dillon had lived at the compound up until last year. He'd gone away to look for a better paying job, but swore he'd come back for her. Despite Savannah's platonic-only feelings for him, he was convinced they'd get married someday. He brushed off her hesitations, telling her they were meant to be together and he was going to take care of her.

Cole turned to her and took her hands, holding them in between his palms. 'Listen. He's not going to find you here. You're safe. Okay?'

She nodded. 'Okay.'

After breakfast Cole announced he was going to the grocery store. 'Is there anything you'd like? You could make a list,' he encouraged, sliding his wallet into the back pocket of his jeans.

'Oh no, you get what you like. I don't want to be a pest.'

'Savannah, you're not.' His look of sincerity stopped any further arguments from her, but she didn't provide him with a list. He didn't want to press it, because even after setting a pad of paper and a pen on the counter, Savannah solemnly shook her head. He didn't know if her refusal was because she really felt like she was overstepping her bounds, or if perhaps she couldn't write; so he let it drop.

At the grocery store his usual routine was to grab just the essentials and juggle everything in his arms. This time though, he wandered down each aisle and practically got one of everything, throwing things into the cart at will. He ventured to the carpeted section of the superstore where there were racks of clothing. Savannah probably needed a few essentials, but he didn't know her size, or what she might like, so he kept walking. He stood in an aisle, looking at the plastic packages of underpants. But damn, buying her panties seemed too forward. He fled, feeling odd even standing in the aisle.

He knew that if she stayed longer, they'd have to cross that bridge and get her more clothes, but not today. Not by himself. He'd have to bring her along next time so she could tell him her size. He didn't allow lovers to stay over, so he didn't have so much as a spare toothbrush in his guest bathroom, so he settled on picking up a toothbrush—something practical, yet still impersonal. He also tossed pink bottles of shampoo and conditioner into his cart before heading for the checkout lanes.

When he got home Savannah was nowhere to be found. Her bedroom door was closed, so he went to work putting away all the groceries, finding that the cabinets were fuller than they had ever been.

When Savannah emerged fifteen minutes later, showered, and once again dressed in the sweats and T-shirt he'd given her last night, he regretted not buying her any clothes. He wondered if she even had panties or a bra under them. He watched her move towards the kitchen and peek inside the cabinets and fridge.

'How'd I do?' he asked, coming up behind her, but bracing himself against the island to keep a physical barrier between them.

'Quite well. I can make lasagna, pot pie, do some baking. This is perfect.'

Cole smiled, glad that he had pleased her. 'I got these for you too.' He pushed the toothbrush, shampoo and conditioner toward her.

Savannah's eyes lit up as she took the bottles in her hands. 'Thank you.' You would have thought he'd given her some elaborate gift. Sure, he splurged a little and bought a brand more expensive than his own cheap shampoo, but he figured she deserved some basic comforts right now. Her whole life had just been turned upside down.

Savannah watched Cole from the corner of her eye, trying to figure out his motivation. *He only wants you for what's between your legs.* Jacob's gruff voice in her head was unwelcome, yet familiar at the same time. What did Cole want with her? Thoughts like that had swirled through her mind since she'd first arrived here. Did he want to touch her? Would he be rough about it, or whisper and caress her sweetly as he touched her? Would she stop him if he tried? Scream and kick and run from the apartment? What would she do then? Maybe she would just let him do what he wanted, take what he wanted. His hands were calloused, but had been gentle when he'd cleaned her wounds, so perhaps it wouldn't be so bad. She could just squeeze her eyes closed and think of something else.

But now it seemed less likely, since he hadn't yet tried to touch her, hadn't laid a single finger on her. And she didn't know what to make of it. Her head felt dizzy with the waiting. At this point she just wanted him to make his move, to get on with it. The waiting and not knowing when he'd strike was exhausting. And so was not knowing how she'd respond.

Being around Cole heightened her senses and left her reeling. She'd never felt this way about Dillon, despite his obvious advances, and found it interesting that even in the presence of Cole's relative distance, her curiosity was piqued and her body at full attention.

She looked down at the pink bottle of shampoo in her hands. She opened the cap and inhaled. Floral notes and the mouth-watering scent of ripe peaches met her senses, and she smiled. She'd used Cole's shampoo that smelled like spearmint and made her scalp tingle, which she liked just fine, but it was nice to have something of her own. Her mouth curved into a slow grin at the thought of Cole picking this out her for. And she relished having conditioner too. Her hair would resemble a bird's nest without it.

After placing the bottles in the guest bathroom, she rejoined Cole in the kitchen to see what she might make for dinner. And perhaps she could even do some baking. As Savannah moved about the kitchen, Cole watched her with suspicion, like he was sure she was about to break down, or freak out at any moment. She didn't feel like crying anymore. She didn't feel much of anything anymore. She just wanted to be sure the kids were okay and figure out her new life, taking one day at a time. She felt relieved more than anything to be free from Jacob and the compound where she'd felt so out of place. And grateful for Cole for giving her a second chance at a life. But being unable to understand his intentions was eating away at her. She couldn't say she was afraid of him; she knew that wasn't it. More like curious about his motives. She felt comfortable enough, dressed in his soft, worn clothing, making herself at home in his kitchen, and most oddly, making herself comfortable in his arms. It was a comfort she needed, and wouldn't deny herself. And after Cole had failed to make any type of move on her last night, she'd grown more comfortable, burrowing into his strong arms on the couch and allowing herself the tiniest semblance of safety, even if it wouldn't last forever.

Chapter 7

Cole awoke suddenly to the sound of a muffled shout. *What the-?*

He was out of bed in an instant and reaching for the handgun he kept in the drawer beside his bed, but then he remembered Savannah. He jogged across the hall and found her thrashing in bed, her arms fighting an imaginary opponent, soft sobs escaping her lips.

'No! No!' she shouted. 'Don't leave me. You can't leave me.' Her voice was filled with so much emotion, such aguish, it nagged at Cole. During the spilt second it took him to cross the room, he wasn't sure if she was talking to him, or still dreaming.

But when he reached the bed and saw the moonlit glow across her face, her eyes were still closed. She was having a nightmare.

'Savannah.' He shook her shoulders. 'Savannah, wake up. It's just a dream.'

Her eyes flashed open and locked on his. 'Cole?'

'Yes, it's Cole, sweetheart, I'm here.'

She reached up for his neck and tugged him down on top of her. Hot tears against his neck kept him from pulling away, like logic demanded he do. Instead his arms snaked around her prone body, and he pulled her even closer. 'Shh. It's okay. I've got you.'

She let out a weak sob and clutched him even tighter, holding on for dear life. After several minutes, her cries had let up, but her death grip on him had not. Knowing that neither of them would get any sleep at this rate, Cole lay down beside her, folding her gently against his body— her back to his front— and wrapped her in his arms. She turned her head and met his eyes, silently begging him not to hurt her. That look just about crushed him. He soothed a hand along her cheek, brushing her messy hair away from her face. He wondered if her dream had been about Dillon, that guy she'd been worried about. 'You're safe. Sleep now.'

His third day off work passed much like the others —he spent the day with Savannah. She cooked. He ate. It was nice, this routine they were developing. Of course he still had no clue what he was doing letting her stay with him. And the longer she stayed, the more likely it was she would discover the skeletons of Cole's past that were better left in the closet. But those thoughts were pushed to the very back of his mind with Savannah's sweet innocence to distract him.

After a dinner of steak, baked potatoes and steamed broccoli, Savannah popped popcorn on the stove and they curled up on the couch to watch a movie. It was a romantic comedy. Savannah leaned forward, curious about the mushy parts, watching the onscreen couple kiss and tumble into bed like she'd never seen anything like it before. Hell, maybe she hadn't.

Cole did his best to try and keep some distance between them, but Savannah inched closer and closer until she was pressed against his side, her head resting on his shoulder. He wanted nothing more than to pull her into his arms and hold her, but the thought was so unwelcome, so unlike him, that he forced himself to sit immobile, and did his best not to notice the beautiful girl beside him. Like that was even possible.

When their movie ended, Cole turned on the news. The first story was about takedown of the cult compound. His eyes flicked to Savannah to measure her reaction, but she'd fallen asleep, her face peaceful and beautiful. He alternated between stealing glances at her sleeping form, and watching the coverage on the compound, but learned nothing new. He waited for the news story to end, and shook her shoulder to wake her. 'Savannah, come on, let's get you in bed.'

She roused, her sleepy eyes blinking up at him. 'No, not yet. I want to stay here with you,' she whispered, her voice raspy from sleep.

She trusted him way too much. She needed to go to her room and probably lock the goddamn door, because the way that T-shirt clung to her tits and crept up her side to expose a taunt patch of skin forced his mind to the gutter. He imagined lifting her shirt over her head and nibbling on her soft flesh, exploring her breasts with gentle licks and kisses until she was moaning out his name in that sweet sleep-laced voice.

He swallowed roughly. 'You need to go to bed. You're falling asleep.'

She met his eyes. 'I don't want to be alone,' she admitted.

He knew he had probably made a mistake by sleeping in the bed with her last night, and he certainly hadn't meant to set a precedent, but knowing he couldn't refuse her request, he simply nodded and led her to his room. His bed was bigger. 'Do you want to sleep in my room?'

'With you?' she asked, her voice rising in uncertainty.

He nodded.

'Yes.'

After they got ready for bed, Cole peeled back the covers and Savannah crawled in. She snuggled into his pillows and inhaled. 'It smells like you.'

He didn't ask if that was good or bad, but the sleepy little smile on her lips confirmed her opinion on the matter. He didn't quite know how to process the fact that his musky scented sheets — that were probably due for a washing — were pleasing to her. He liked her scent too, though. Maybe it was only natural to be attracted to the scent of the opposite sex.

Cole knew this was dangerous ground. Not just because he was undeniably attracted to her, but because he was afraid that he was making himself too vital in her life. She certainly couldn't stay here long-term, and then what? He never intended for her to grow attached to him. Yet that was exactly what seemed to be happening. Cole changed in the bathroom, stripping off his shirt and stepping into the pajama pants he'd begun wearing for Savannah's benefit.

When he crawled into bed in the dimly lit room, Savannah inched toward him and nestled in against his bare chest. The soft curve of her breast pressed against the firm plain of his chest, and her legs tangled with his. He went instantly hard. *Fuck*.

He sat up and removed her grasp on him. 'No, Savannah. You can't do that. You can sleep in here if you want, but I need my space.'

She bit her lip and looked down, seemingly hurt at being scolded.

'Hey, it's okay. You didn't do anything wrong. I'm just used to sleeping on my own.' It was the truth, but not entirely. He wanted nothing more to take her in his arms and hold her all night. Hell, if he was admitting it to himself, he wanted to do a lot more than that to her tempting little body, though he'd never let himself act on it. He would not take advantage of her that way, but mostly he just didn't want her to discover he was hard.

Savannah's tortured gaze caught his in the moonlight. 'Are you mad at me?'

He couldn't resist stroking her cheek. 'No. You didn't do anything wrong. Just get some rest, okay?'

She nodded, and lay back down — this time on the other side of the king-sized bed. She found his hand under the blankets and gave it a squeeze. 'Thank you, Cole.'

He rubbed his thumb over the back of her hand, enjoying the simple contact between them. 'Good night, Savannah, sleep well.' A few moments later, her breathing became deep and even, and he knew she'd fallen asleep. He was much too keyed up to do the same. His erection begged for attention. And having her soft, feminine curves right there next to him was pressing all his buttons. He glanced at the door to the master bath, wondering if he could slip out of bed silently and go jerk off. But if Savannah woke up and called for him, then what? He took a deep breath and let it out slowly, knowing he'd get no relief tonight.

Cole shot up straight up in bed and cursed. The room was dark and silent. He urged his heart to slow the fuck down before he got up and punched something.

'Cole?' Savannah rubbed at her eyes and sat up next to him.

Fuck. He'd forgotten about Savannah. But apparently his subconscious hadn't. The dreams were eerily reminiscent of how he met her.

She placed a hand on his back, resting between his shoulder blades. 'Are you okay?'

'Don't touch me.' He shrugged out of her grasp. He knew trying to sleep would be pointless now that he'd dreamed of *her*. Cole climbed out of bed. He put on gym shorts, stripping his pajama pants in the dark, and added a T-shirt. Savannah was up and out of bed and behind him, wrapping her arms around his back so her hands locked together around his waist. Her breasts rasped through the thin cotton of the T-shirt she wore and pressed against his back.

'Dammit, Savannah.' He peeled her hands off him and turned to face her. 'Let me go.' He didn't need her tenderness right now. It would only make things worse once she understood. 'There are things you don't know about me.'

They stood staring at each other in the pre-dawn light. Her gaze registered surprise and hint of fear. He knew she'd never seen this side of him, hadn't even imagined it existed. God, he wished it didn't. But the sad truth was, he'd fucked up big time. He just hoped she never knew the extent of it. It struck him how little they each knew about one another, yet how easily they'd fallen into this routine together.

He reached out and squeezed her hand to show her that he wasn't mad. 'Just go back to bed. I'm going to the gym.'

She glanced at the clock beside the bed. It was four a.m., but she didn't argue, she just nodded and climbed back in the bed, curling up in the warmth of the spot he'd just vacated.

Chapter 8

'Okay, so no questions, no objections. You're going,' Marissa pressed.

Cole dragged the phone from his ear, blowing out a sigh. 'I don't know, Marissa, I've been pretty busy with work lately.' She didn't need to know that he was currently on vacation.

'Oh Colby, you're gonna love her. I met Sali in my yoga class. She's gorgeous, fun. Close to your age. I really think you'll like her. How long's it been since you've been on a date?'

Fuck. The last thing he wanted to do as go on some blind date, but even more than that, he didn't want to get Marissa pissed at him, because if he did, she was likely to come over to give him a piece of her mind and then she'd find Savannah here.

Marissa had been urging him to use dating websites, but he'd adamantly refused. He'd rather get a quick lay than have to sit and listen to a girl he wasn't interested in prattle on about how her last manicure was chipping after only two days — no joke, that was the actual dinner conversation of his last date.

But with his second to last single friend getting married that past summer, Cole was beginning to realize it might be time to look for a good girl. He just wasn't good at dating. He never seemed to meet the expectations women had. He was forgetful, he wasn't romantic, and he worked too much. He didn't know many girls that would take him the way he was, but he didn't want to be someone's project. He wasn't changing. Hell, he even pissed Marissa off and she was family — she had to love him.

'I arranged it so that you guys could meet at Liam's,' Marissa said. 'You're there every weekend anyway, so what's the big deal?'

Marissa had a point. His best friend Liam owned an Irish pub practically walking distance from his condo. 'Fine, I'll go,' he muttered into the phone. Since Marissa regularly threatened to create an online dating profile for him, he occasionally complied to keep her off his back. 'Sali, huh?'

'Yes! Okay, well I already arranged everything. You guys are meeting two weeks from Saturday at seven for drinks. That's it. Simple, huh?'

'Okay.'

'Would it kill you to thank your sister?'

'Thanks, Rissa.' He rolled his eyes before ending the call. It was still a couple weeks away, maybe he could find a way out of it.

The following day, before heading to the gym, Cole dropped Savannah off at her therapy appointment that had been pre-scheduled by the facility coordinator. After a vigorous workout and a quick shower, Cole was dressed and back in his SUV, headed to pick up Savannah.

He entered the doctor's office, took a seat in the reception area, and began flipping through a magazine. A few minutes later, the office door opened and Savannah emerged with swollen eyes. Cole sprung to his feet.

The doctor stepped around Savannah towards Cole. 'Is this him?'

Savannah nodded, her eyes locked on Cole's.

Christ, this wasn't good. He could get in trouble with the Bureau for even being here with her. The doctor, mid-forties with graying hair at his temples, strode toward Cole and extended his hand. 'I'm Doctor White, but call me Malcolm. Do you mind if we have a word, Cole?'

Cole nodded. It was the only thing he could do, though he was confused and on edge. What had Savannah told her therapist about him?

As soon as they were seated in his large office, Malcolm cut to the chase. 'She told me who you were. But don't worry—doctor / patient confidentially and all that. Plus I don't care who you work for. I get the sense that you want to help Savannah, so I wanted to offer some guidance.'

Cole leaned forward, his hands on his knees, ready to listen to whatever the doctor had to say. It seemed that they were on the same page. This was about Savannah.

'These sessions will help, but they're only once a week. Savannah needs to get into a regular routine. She needs some semblance of normal in her life.'

Cole nodded in agreement. No shit, doc. That's the brilliant advice he probably charges three-hundred dollars an hour to deliver?

'She seems to have a caring, nurturing spirit.'

Cole recognized as much; she loved to cook and seemed content to feed him and stay at home. But he waited, wondering where this conversation was heading.

'She needs someone or something to care for. Do you have pets, plants, anything?'

'Ah, no.' Cole scrubbed a hand over his scruff.

'So it seems at the moment what she's putting her caring energy into is you. That concerns me.' Malcolm frowned. 'Savannah could grow quite attached at this vulnerable point in her life. You'll need to be careful.'

If the doc felt it necessary, he'd buy her a plant, but he didn't see how watering a cactus once a week would help. Not to mention he was enjoying Savannah funneling her nurturing energy into taking care of him. 'Got any advice for me?' Cole asked, shifting in the stiff leather chair. He didn't like admitting that he had no clue what he was doing, but he needed the advice, and since Savannah had already told the doctor about him, there was no use pretending he wasn't involved.

Dr. Malcolm White laced his fingers in front of his round stomach. 'Watch for withdrawn or self-destructive behaviors. She didn't have the normal teenage experience, and even though she's wise beyond her years, it's possible she could go through a late rebellious stage — wanting to experience the typical teenage things she missed out on.'

'Okay…' Cole wasn't sure what he meant, but he thought of his own rebellious years… sneaking out to go to parties, drinking too much, getting in fights and fooling around with girls he had no intention of dating. He couldn't see Savannah behaving like that. She seemed too sweet, too innocent.

'And there's one other thing…' The doctor swallowed and met his eyes. 'She's not ready for any type of romantic relationship, physical or otherwise. I don't know what your interests in her are, but…'

Cole held up a hand, stopping him there. 'I have zero interest in starting a relationship with her. And as far as anything physical… she's just a kid.'

The doctor frowned. 'I wouldn't say that. She'll be twenty in a couple of months, more than old enough for a relationship; I just don't think she's ready yet. She's got a lot of healing to do first.'

Cole nodded. 'Listen, like I said, I'm not interested in that with her.'

'She's an attractive girl. I had to bring it up.'

Cole didn't respond. He couldn't. His voice, along with his self-assuredness had disappeared. The truth was he had no idea what he was doing with Savannah. Not a clue. But he knew one thing; he felt a compelling need to keep her safe. He'd just have to shut off any attraction he felt for her.

He accepted a stack of self-help books from Dr. White, unsure if they were for Savannah or him, and stalked from the office.

Chapter 9

'Do you mind if we turn on the TV?' Savannah asked. 'It's just so quiet in here, and I'm used to more background noise.'

'Sure.' Cole handed her the remote, and she stared down at it curiously like it was some strange foreign object. 'Here.' He hit the power button, bringing the flat screen to life.

It was turned to one of the premium channels, which thankfully kept the programming clean during the day. He rarely watched TV, but when he did, it was typically when he couldn't sleep and it was either watch the soft-core smut on this channel, or infomercials. And a man only needed so many Shark Vacuums and Ab Rollers.

Savannah studied the TV for a moment, wincing at the string of curse words that ripped from the foul-mouthed character on screen. Cole quickly changed the station. The Weather Channel. That was a safe enough option.

Savannah smiled at him in appreciation and headed back into the kitchen.

A short while later, she hesitated at the threshold of the living room, a casserole dish in her hands. 'I made beef wellington, would you like some?'

She couldn't have known that was his favorite and his mother used to make it for him on special occasions. 'You made wellington?'

She nodded. 'It's my favorite.'

'Mine too.'

All that week Savannah had made elaborate meals for Cole. Eggs benedict for breakfast, panini sandwiches for lunch, that afternoon she'd baked and decorated six dozen sugar cookies, and now it was beef wellington. She didn't know how to make the right portions for just two of them either, so leftovers were stacked in both the fridge and freezer. He'd have meals for the next year at this rate.

Malcolm's words rang in his head…*Savannah's the nurturing type…she needs to get in a healthy routine…* He wasn't sure all this cooking counted as a healthy routine. She rarely left the kitchen, and when she did, she didn't know what to do with herself.

Cole was still full from lunch, but he forced down a few bites of the delicious meal, praising Savannah for her efforts. He noticed that she barely ate any of the food she cooked, like she was doing it solely for his benefit. He decided it was time to act.

Cole returned an hour later, wondering if he had made the right decision. The puppy wiggled in his arms, anxious to get down and play. *Crap*. What if Savannah didn't even like dogs, or what if she was allergic? Deciding it was too late to turn back now, Cole unlocked the door and went inside.

Not seeing Savannah, he carried the Maltese-Poodle puppy toward her bedroom and knocked at the door. 'Savannah?'

He heard her sniffle. 'Just a second.'

The puppy let out a whimper and reached out a paw toward the door scratching to get in, like it somehow knew it's mother was inside. Savannah slowly opened the door. A smile lighting up her tear-streaked face. 'Cole?' She blinked, an unspoken question forming on her lips.

'She's for you. She's fourteen weeks old. A family bought her from a pet store, and then changed their mind and dropped her off at the shelter down the road. She's yours. If you want her.'

'Oh, Cole.' Savannah lifted up on her toes and pressed a kiss to his cheek. 'Thank you. She's so cute.'

Cole handed the squirming thing over to Savannah, who promptly kissed the top of its head and cradled it on her hip like a baby. She captured his attention and held it. Cole's lips turned up in satisfaction as he watched the touching sight.

There was no denying the dog was cute. She was a whopping six pounds of fluffy cream and tan fur, with a tail that wagged non-stop. Cole wanted to adopt a German Shepherd, or some other manly dog, but when he saw this little thing that looked more like a gremlin than a dog, he knew it was the one Savannah would want. And if the way Savannah buried her face in the puppy's fur and murmured unintelligible baby talk to it was any indication, he'd done the right thing. His heart squeezed in his chest — the feeling unfamiliar and startling. But he reminded himself he'd only done this to get her doctor off his back. Animal therapy or some shit it was called.

'What are you going to name her?' he asked.

Savannah's lips curved into a smile. God she was beautiful when she smiled. 'I get to name her?'

He nodded and watched her eyes light up.

'I'll have to think about it.' She smiled, holding the puppy out at arm's length to get a good look at her.

Cole left again with the excuse of needing to pick up a collar, leash and dog food. But mostly, he needed to escape the over-whelming feelings brought on by Savannah's sweet murmurings to the puppy.

Chapter 10

'Come here, Cuddles.' Savannah scooped the fluff ball up from the floor and balanced the dog on her hip. 'That's a good girl. No biting Cole.'

The damn dog had turned out to be an ankle biter — often nipping at Cole's heels as he walked across the apartment.

'Dammit, that hurt you little beast.' Cole absently rubbed his tender Achilles tendon.

Savannah didn't scold the dog, just picked it up and lovingly stroked its back. No wonder the thing was so naughty. She let it get away with murder. Of course, it was only naughty towards Cole. Cuddles treated Savannah as though she walked on water. Probably because she was the one who fed and walked it. Cole usually looked at it with suspicion and distrust.

Now that Savannah had Cuddles and was starting to adjust, Cole decided his forced vacation was over. He was going back to work. Norm would just have to deal with the fact that it was two days early. Savannah had settled in better than he could have expected, and the dog had helped a lot.

Cole had shown her the grassy fenced in area where tenants could exercise their dogs. He showed her the little bags for cleaning up after Cuddles, and gave her an extra key to his condo, telling her to make sure she kept the door locked. She didn't seem too upset by the thought of him going to work, which was good. She asked if she could take a bubble bath in the sunken tub in his master bath, and said she wanted to read some of the books Dr. White had given her too.

When he arrived at the office the next morning, Norm grumbled something unintelligible and several of the guys groaned, and then began swapping money. *What the-?*

Instead of ordering him back on vacation, like he suspected would happen, Norm patted him on the back. 'Good work. You stayed away longer than I thought you would.'

He looked around at the grinning faces of his co-workers. 'You guys took bets on me?'

'Most had you coming back on Tuesday. I had today, which means you just won me fifty bucks.' Norm grinned. 'Now everyone back to work.' He shoved a file of printouts at Cole. 'Here's a new case for you.'

Regardless of their jabs, Cole knew being back at work was a good thing. It would help give him some much needed perspective and occupy his brain, hopefully forcing thoughts of Savannah aside, if only for eight hours at a time.

When he got home from work, he found Savannah sitting on the living room floor clutching Cuddles to her chest, tears freely streaming down her cheeks.

He dropped his bag in the entryway and stormed across the living room, falling to his knees in front of her. 'Savannah, what is it? What happened?' He cradled her jaw in his hands, meeting her teary eyes.

She looked at him and then back at the TV. 'Oh Cole, it's just so sad.'

He looked at the screen to see what she'd been watching. It was one of those damn talk shows that featured a cast of low lives — this episode appeared to be a girl who didn't know who the father of their baby was. A tattooed guy strutted across the stage, shouting obscenities at the audience after learning he was not the father. The mother was not to be outdone, was wildly gesturing and shouting, nearly every word bleeped out.

Cole turned it off. 'You shouldn't be watching that trash.'

'She didn't know who the father of her child was, and he was just so mean...' She sniffed, drawing a deep breath. 'And the poor baby...'

Cole pulled her to his chest. 'Shh, it's not real. It's just TV.' He didn't know if that was entirely true, but Savannah didn't need to know that. She was just too vulnerable, too impressionable, having not grown up in the real world. If he could protect her from even some of its harsh realities, he would.

After holding her for a few minutes until her tears subsided, Cole rubbed gentle circles on her back. She pulled away and met his eyes. Still red and puffy, but no fresh tears. 'Are you okay?'

She nodded, unwilling to take her eyes from his. 'Thanks for... everything. For taking care of me.'

Her lips were only a few inches from his. The desire to kiss her was an overwhelming need, sucking the air from his lungs. His breathing became shallow and he nodded, still meeting her eyes.

She smiled softly and rose to her feet, leaving Cole sitting on his living room rug alone. After shaking away the crazy thoughts in his head, everything from a fierce surge of protectiveness to attraction, he got up and joined Savannah in the kitchen.

He sat perched on a stool while she began dinner. As she cooked, Savannah asked about his day at work. He told her about his new case, investigating a man who was believed to be working with a known terrorist. She listened in rapt interest as she sautéed chicken and vegetables for stir fry. He couldn't help but notice how comfortable it felt to come home to Savannah at night, rather than his empty apartment. And a hot meal too? He knew he could get used to this — and that was bad, very bad.

*

Gasping for air, Savannah untangled herself from the sheets and fought to get her breathing under control. It was just a dream. Dillon wasn't there. Jacob was gone. And she was safe. Tell that to her heart, currently thundering in her chest like she'd just sprinted a marathon.

'Savannah? What is it?' Cole sat up in bed, running a hand across his face.

'Sorry, nothing. Just a bad dream,' she mumbled. 'I didn't mean to wake you.'

Cole reached over and flicked on the small bedside lamp. Savannah blinked against the warm glow, finding Cole's features etched in concern and his hair rumpled from sleep.

Placing his warm palm on the center of her back, he rubbed slow circles, working to calm her. Savannah drew a slow shuddering breath and attempted a smile, trying to show him she wasn't as broken as she felt.

'What was the dream about?' he asked, his voice thick with sleep.

Blinking a few times, her eyes adjusted to the light and Savannah took notice of Cole's shirtless form. His broad bare chest was enough of a distraction, and she focused on him instead of the memories swirling in her head. 'It was just something that happened a few weeks before the raid. Dillon sat me down and explained that his father had promised him that I could be his. That was why he needed to go away and work, to save up money for our future.'

Cole's brow wrinkled and his hand stilled on her back. 'What do you mean *promised you could be his*?'

Savannah shrugged. She knew she didn't want to belong to anyone. She wanted to be her own woman, and be loved and cherished in her own right, but free to come and go, make her own choices. Living with Jacob, or Dillon for that matter, that wasn't possible. Which was why she was so grateful for Cole. She kept most of these somber memories to herself, preferring instead to focus on the good things — like the children and the few friends she'd had there. But she couldn't control her subconscious, and dreams of Jacob's crazy rants and Dillon urgings needed to stop.

'Can you just hold me tonight?' she whispered to Cole.

His expression was guarded, but he nodded his consent and held open his arms. Savannah crawled closer, nestled herself into the crook of his arm and he lowered them both to the bed, reaching over to flip off the light. Savannah breathed in his warm, male scent and rested her head against the firm plane of his chest. As crazy as it was, she felt completely safe and at ease with Cole. She took a deep breath and closed her eyes, slipping into a restful sleep in Cole's solid embrace.

That Sunday Cole got changed and readied himself for a tough conversation. He ventured to the living room and found Savannah on the sofa, little magazine clippings on the coffee table in front of her like she was in the middle of some project.

'I have this thing I do on Sundays,' he started.

Savannah looked up him curiously, Cuddles dozing near her hip. 'Okay.' She turned back to her magazine cutouts — pictures of puppies and babies, and other nonsensical things.

'I'll um, be back before dinner.'

She nodded.

He slipped into his shoes, still waiting for her questions, but they never came.

Savannah didn't say a thing. Didn't even raise an eyebrow about where he went on Sundays. What would he say if she did? How would he explain his relationship with Abbie? Perhaps it was best to shield Savannah from the whole situation, including his messy relationship history. Things were manageable now. Two hours on a Sunday were all that was required to keep things running smoothly. And so far, Savannah hadn't asked a single question. Perhaps it was one of those things better left unknown. Easier for all involved. He was trying to do the right thing by Abbie. Of course, now that Savannah was in his life, things had gotten considerably more complicated. He didn't normally do complicated.

Cole had always felt confident in his decision to maintain his relationship with Abbie. He was doing the right thing to help a friend in need — simple as that. Then why did it feel like a fuck of a lot more suddenly? The fact that Savannah didn't know about her turned it into some dirty secret. He had enough skeletons in his closet, and he didn't particularly enjoy adding another. But he drew in a deep breath and shook off the tension building between his shoulder blades. Just because he had Savannah in his life didn't mean he could walk away from his other responsibilities.

Cole ran his hands over his face, pressing the heels of his palms over his eyes. Why women didn't come with an instruction manual was beyond him.

Chapter 11

Monday morning came too quickly after another pleasant weekend spent with Cole. Savannah yawned and smoothed her hair back, securing it in a low ponytail at the nape of her neck. The least she could do to say thank you was to help out around the house, not to mention if they wanted to eat, the responsibility seemed to rest on her. 'The coffee's ready,' she called to Cole.

He entered the kitchen with a frown. 'Not in the mood.'

He always drank coffee. Always. 'What's wrong?' she asked, turning to watch him fasten the last few buttons on his dress shirt. She helped him with the cufflinks that his fingers always stumbled over. 'Here. Let me.'

'Thanks.' He smiled weakly.

'Are you sick?' she asked, noticing the dark circles beneath his eyes.

'It's just an upset stomach. I'll be fine.'

She stared at him, having never seen him under the weather, and felt altogether useless. 'Can I get you some ginger ale and soda crackers?'

He nodded. 'Ah, sure. Maybe that'll do the trick.' He slipped into his loafers while Savannah poured a small glass of the bubbly amber-colored drink. 'My mom used to give me the same thing.'

'Here.' She watched while he munched down the crackers and then downed the soda.

'See, I'm fine Savannah.' He chuckled, passing back the empty glass.

'Okay,' she said reluctantly, accepting it. He'd done so much for her, it was the least she could do to be there for him. Savannah headed into the kitchen and switched off the coffee maker, having never developed a taste for the stuff herself, and watched from the corner of her eye as Cole stuffed his cell phone, wallet and keys into the pockets of his slacks. He was a man of routine, that much was certain. He kept all his essentials, plus some loose change, and a seldom worn watch in a small mahogany box on his entryway table, and repeated this same ritual each morning. Savannah continued to inspect him, appreciating the way he looked dressed up in his work clothes, when Cole suddenly darted from the entryway, passing her as he shot down the hall.

'Cole…' She followed him toward the bathroom, but the sounds of him becoming sick stopped her at the threshold. She stood with her back pressed against the wall just outside the bathroom door, wondering if she should go to him.

She heard the water running and him gargling. 'Cole?' she knocked softly on the door. 'Are you okay?'

'I'll be out in a minute,' he called. His voice was tense and rougher than usual, making Savannah's stomach knot with worry.

He emerged a second later, looking no worse for the wear and continued past her to the front door. 'See you tonight.'

'Cole!' She met him at the door. 'You're still going to work?'

He nodded, pausing at the half-open front door. 'Yeah.'

'But you were just sick!'

'So? I'm a big boy. I'll be fine.'

'You have the flu; go get in bed.'

An expression of surprise crossed Cole's face and he darted for the bathroom, cursing under his breath. She heard the telltale signs of him getting sick again.

A few minutes later, Savannah steered Cole into his bedroom, refusing to take no for an answer, and helped him step out of his dress slacks, pockets still full and belt dangling loosely.

'I need my cell.' He looked adorably cute standing there pouting in just his black boxers briefs and white undershirt.

Slightly exasperated that he was going to be a difficult patient, Savannah anchored her hands on her hips, ready to do what it took to force him into being an obedient patient. 'No phones. No work. No.'

'I'm just going to send Norm a text and tell him I'm staying home today.'

She bit her lip, deciding if she could believe him. 'Fine.' She handed over his cell phone and went to hang his slacks in the closet. From inside the closet, she heard him mumbling to himself that *criminals don't take a day off and neither should he.*

She returned to his bedside and was ready to forcibly remove the phone from his hands, but as he promised, he sent one quick text, then set the phone on the bedside table. He rolled to his side, hugged a pillow to his chest and closed his eyes.

She pushed his hair back from his forehead, feeling for a temperature. She secretly loved how his hair looked when he first woke up, like a rakish young boy who'd been out all night raising trouble, or enjoying a tumble between the sheets. She pressed the back of her hand against his cheek and his eyes fluttered open. 'You feel warm,' she whispered.

'Mmm,' he groaned.

'Think you can keep down some water?'

He nodded.

Savannah returned with a glass of chilled water and two pain relievers, which she set on the bedside table for later once she was confident he was done getting sick. Cole's foggy gaze met hers, watching as she arranged the blankets around him and fussed over him. She tipped the glass of water to his lips and he swallowed a tiny sip, before dropping his head back to the pillow again.

'Thanks,' he croaked, his voice raw. 'Lay with me?' he asked softly. He'd never requested her presence before, never acted like it mattered. They'd cuddled and lain together so many times, but it was always at her urging. Her heart thumped in her chest at hearing him ask for her in that way. It was just because he was sick. But that didn't mean she wasn't allowed to enjoy it all the same.

She pulled back the covers, joining him in between the sheets where she could snuggle up properly. Cole cracked open one eye and lifted his arm, urging her nearer.

'Get closer, I'm cold,' he whispered.

His skin felt hot to the touch, but Savannah didn't argue, draping her arm across his chest, and one leg over his hips as she wrapped her body around his.

He sighed a little sound of contentment and pressed a kiss to her hair. 'Thanks, Savannah.'

Savannah awoke to an intense heat radiating around her. She flung the blankets off her, gasping for breath. God he was burning up. 'Cole?' She shook his shoulders trying to rouse him. 'Cole, wake up.'

He lazily opened one eye and let out a slight groan. 'Need Savannah.' His hand raised and then flopped heavily against the mattress.

'I am Savannah. Sit up so you can take some pain reliever for me.'

'No...want Savannah,' he groaned, his eyes still closed.

She reached for the pills, pried open Cole's lips and placed them on his tongue, then patted his cheeks and made him take a sip of water. He did so, lethargically, before falling back against his pillow.

'Savannah...' he breathed once more.

She smoothed her hands through his hair. 'Shh. Just rest. I'm here.' She rubbed his neck and shoulders, finding them tense even while he slept.

Hope surged in her chest. Feeling needed and vital was a sentiment that she missed so much it brought tears to her eyes. She blinked them away and brought a palm to Cole's roughened cheek, skittering her thumb back and forth. *He only needs you because he's delirious with fever.* She ignored the empty feeling in her chest and continued smoothing his hair back and gently caressing him, doing her best to soothe both of their aches.

Chapter 12

Having recovered from the twenty-four hour flu, Cole was back at work the following day. He'd spent the week working on a new case, but had hit a lull. He stretched at his desk, his neck cracking with the movement and decided to check into the cult case to see if there was anything new. He also wanted to learn more about Dillon.

He typed a search into the database and hit enter. He learned that all fourteen children had been reunited with their mothers —none of whom were charged in the case. He knew that would make Savannah happy. He thought about going home mid-day to check on her, but talked himself out of it.

There was surprising little about Dillon. He'd been tracked to Amarillo where he was working manual labor. He's been given the news of his father's death and was also questioned at that time, but the interview didn't reveal much.

Cole continued perusing the file and stumbled across a photo of Dillon. It was a candid shot from his time at the compound, and Savannah was in the photo too, sitting on his knee in front of a rustic fire pit — a wide smile on her face. The picture ate away at him. Maybe she really was happy living there. Sure, she seemed to be adjusting well to staying with him, but seeing the pure bliss on her face — under a darkened, star filled sky, seated with friends and family next to her — he began to realize there was more to her life at the compound than crazy Jacob.

He studied the picture closer. Dillon's hands rested on Savannah's hip and his face was covered in a stupid ass grin. If this bastard so much as laid one finger on Savannah, he'd personally castrate the son of bitch. He considered how to bring up Dillon to Savannah to get more information about their relationship, but decided to proceed with caution. She was doing so well, he didn't want to upset her. Savannah had seemed somewhat worried and hesitant to discuss Dillon, so at least for now, he'd let it drop. Savannah was safe. That's all that mattered.

He knew he couldn't just keep her holed up in his condo, even if he wanted to. He realized that in the weeks Savannah had been staying with him, she'd yet to leave the house, aside from her therapy appointments and walking the dog. It was Friday night, and he decided that tonight that would change. If Savannah really was going to be staying with him, he wanted to do all he could to help re-acclimate her to her new life. Step one to her gaining some confidence and independence was to get out of his condo on a regular basis. Her three times a day trips to take Cuddles outside didn't count, though he supposed that was a start.

He would take her out to dinner — give her a break from cooking. Of course she would need something to wear, other than his oversized sweats and T-shirts she seemed comfortable in.

Looking up from his computer screen at a rustling noise next to him, he spotted agent Amanda Larson shuffling through her desk drawer. He'd never really paid her much attention before. They rarely worked together, though he knew she was good at her job.

'Colby Fletcher,' she scolded. 'Were you just checking out my backside?' She turned to face him, placing her hands on her hips.

His eyes darted up to hers. He had been, but not for the reason she seemed to think.

She appeared to be about the same size as Savannah. 'What size are you?'

Her playful grin instantly evaporated. 'You never ask a girl her size. God, no wonder you're still single.'

He wasn't sure how she knew that fact about him, or what exactly she meant by the statement — well actually he did — that he was insensitive. And he couldn't argue with that. But the thing was, he knew that Savannah was changing him little by little. 'I need to buy a gift, and you look about the right size. Can you just help me out here?'

'Fine.' She frowned. 'Size four petite pants. A small or medium on the top.'

Cole scribbled down the information on a piece of paper and stuffed it in his pocket.

When Cole got home from work, his house was strangely silent. He set the shopping bags down on the island and searched for Savannah. Not finding either her or Cuddles, he ventured outside, not bothering to change from his work clothes. He found Savannah, but not at all like he had expected. Though he guessed he knew better than to expect anything normal from her.

She was sitting cross-legged in the grass next to the guy from unit 4D, Levi something or other. Her head was thrown back and the sweet sound of her laughter tumbled from her lips.

What the fuck?

Levi was casually leaning back on his elbow, plucking at a blade of grass. Cole couldn't hear what Levi was saying, but whatever it was, he was sure he had never seen Savannah so carefree or laughing with such abandon. Something inside him clenched with jealousy. Savannah was his. He didn't know where that thought had come from, but there it was, insistent and possessive.

Levi's head snapped up once Cole got closer, and Savannah's laugh died on her lips when she saw his expression. He was sure he looked ready to kill someone. Well not just someone — the asshole from 4D, specifically.

'Whoa there FBI man,' Levi chuckled, straightening his spine at the implied threat in Cole's posture.

'Savannah?' His voice was low, rougher than he intended.

Savannah scrambled to her feet. 'Cole?'

He closed his eyes and took a deep breath, forcing himself to calm down. Savannah approached him carefully and placed a hand on his forearm, which worked to relax him.

'You weren't inside,' he bit out in a clipped tone.

'Cuddles needed to go potty.' She lifted the dog onto her hip, her eyes full of worry.

He nodded. 'Everything's fine.' He patted the top of Cuddles' head, and rubbed his thumb across Savannah's cheek. Watching her laughing and looking at Levi had set something off inside him. 'Go on inside. I got a surprise for you tonight. The bags on the counter are for you. Get changed. We're going out.'

'Out?' she choked on the word.

He nodded. 'Go on. I'll be up in a sec.' He couldn't ease her mind about going out just yet, he needed to deal with Levi first. He was sniffing around Savannah like a damn dog and he was about to learn that was not okay.

The only things Cole knew about Levi were that he was twenty years old, went to the local community college and lived with his mother, a forty-something divorcee who had come on to Cole on more than one occasion.

Once Savannah had disappeared inside, Cole turned to face Levi, stepping in closer until they were chest to chest.

Cole's intense gaze penetrated Levi's and he shook his head slowly. 'She's off-limits.'

Levi didn't falter. 'She's a little young for you, isn't she?'

'That's none of your fucking business. I'm only going to say this once. Stay away from her.'

Levi scrubbed a hand over his stubble-covered jaw. 'Whatever you say man, chill out. We were just talking.'

Cole let out a huff and stalked back inside. Shit. Maybe he shouldn't have freaked out on Levi. Savannah was allowed to have friends, after all. But there was just something that didn't sit well with the thought of her having male friends. Still he knew he had no right to be mad at Savannah. He'd have to work on that.

Chapter 13

Savannah carried the shopping bags into the guest bathroom. She removed each item to inspect it. A pair of dark-washed stretchy jeans, a heather gray sweater that was super soft and thin, and a pair of white cotton panties. She brought the clothes to her face and inhaled. Mmm. They smelled new, like a department store. She'd rarely had new clothes bought just for her, having worn hand-me-downs most of her life. She quickly changed and threw the sweats into the bathroom hamper.

When she turned toward the mirror, she stared at her reflection in disbelief. The clothes fit perfectly —the jeans sat low on her waist, hugging her hips and bottom, and the top was so fine and soft, she couldn't resist wrapping her arms around herself for a squeeze. She felt pretty for the first time in a long time, and she had Cole to thank. Awareness of her growing debt to him prickled at the back of her mind. She owed him for Cuddles, and now the new clothes.

She finger-combed her dark hair and glanced at her reflection one last time before going to find Cole. He was sitting on a barstool at the kitchen island, drinking a bottle of beer. With only his profile in view, Cole hadn't yet noticed her. Savannah took a moment to study him uninterrupted. She had come to love just looking at him when she knew he wasn't watching. His back and shoulders were powerful with muscles that bunched under his shirt. Even his forearms were masculine —she could see where he'd pushed his sleeves up and thick veins strained against his arms. He was beautiful, yet ruggedly masculine. He was her safety, her comfort. She owed him everything. But she had no idea how to repay him.

She straightened her shoulders and cleared her throat. Cole turned toward her, the bottle of beer suspended halfway to his lips. His eyes began at her denim-clad thighs, and moved slowly over her hips, her flat belly, up to her chest and lingered there a moment before finally settling on her eyes. He didn't try to hide the fact that he was checking her out, and made no apologies for his behavior. Savannah squirmed under his gaze. She was amazed that one look could make her feel hot all over and so feminine at the same time. Without dropping his gaze from hers, he dragged the bottle of beer to his lips and pulled down a healthy swig, his throat moving with the effort.

'Thank you for the clothes,' Savannah offered, needing to break the heavy silence that hung between them.

'They fit,' he murmured, his eyes still refusing to leave hers.

She blushed and looked down, suddenly realizing that he had shopped for her, picked these things out, even the panties that now seemed to accentuate the throb in her groin. She pulled in a deep breath and headed for the kitchen, unable to stand on display for his perusal any longer. She retrieved his empty bottle of beer and rinsed it in the sink before adding it to the recycling bin under the sink.

Cole was right behind her when she turned, holding her captive against the counter with his large form. She never felt frightened of him, more like intrigued. But she was always aware of where he was in relation to her, and how large and masculine he was physically. And at this exact moment, dressed in nice clothes that he had taken the time to pick for her, she felt womanly, soft and pretty next to his raw masculinity.

'Cole?' She looked up, meeting his dark eyes.

'Damn, Savannah, when I saw you talking to Levi…' he trailed off, resting a heavy hand on her hip. The weight of his warm hand surprised her, and her lungs refused to cooperate. 'I didn't like it,' he admitted, staring at her point blank.

Her stomach dropped. Savannah wouldn't do anything to upset him. Couldn't. He was everything she had right now. 'I'm, I'm sorry,' she stammered.

'No.' Cole stepped in closer, until his thighs were pressed against hers, and their faces were just inches apart. They had touched many times, but not like this — not when Cole was angry and rough, his gaze filled with intensity. Warning bells went off in Savannah's head. She gripped the counter behind her. 'You should be able to talk to whoever you want without me getting all possessive.'

'Oh.' Savannah was at a complete loss, having never experienced this type of relationship with a man before. He seemed angry, but more so at himself than her. She wasn't sure what to do, so she remained completely still. His hand tightened on her hip, clutching her close to him. And his other hand cupped her cheek as he leaned in closer. For a second Savannah thought he might kiss her and her heart jumped into her throat. She held her breath, waiting, but he only stroked her jaw lovingly with his thumb. 'You look nice,' he whispered, before dropping his hands and moving away.

The loss of his body near hers was almost painful. Somehow in the past few weeks Savannah had begun to crave his physical contact, and when he wasn't near, it left an ache that settled over her skin and inside her chest. But before she had time to dwell on any of that, Cole led her to the door and ushered her outside.

They rode to the restaurant with the music playing low. Cole turned the radio on scan and told her to stop at whichever station she liked. She frowned at the heavy metal, twang-y country and hip hop music, but when she heard the soulful voice of a woman, she leaned forward in her seat and asked Cole to leave it. It was someone named Lana Del Rey, he said. They listened to her sing about blue jeans, big dreams and love that lasted a million years. Savannah listened to the words, saying a silent prayer that love like that was real and would find her in this crazy world.

They arrived at the restaurant — a bistro type place that served the best wood-fired pizzas, Cole said.

When they stepped inside, Savannah noticed the restaurant was small, but upscale, decorated in reds, browns and creams. It was dimly lit and had a cozy, rustic feel.

The entrance was filled with people waiting for tables. Savannah wasn't used to being in crowds of strangers, but the feel of Cole's fingertips against her lower back soothed her. She crossed the room toward a long dark bar, lit with tiny lamps every few feet.

'Is this okay?' He motioned for her to have a seat on the stool he'd pulled out for her. 'I usually come by myself and sit up here. You don't have to wait, plus you can watch the action in the kitchen.' He motioned to the large wood-burning oven that looked more like a fireplace. She took the stool and could immediately see why Cole liked to sit there. Watching the cooks work, stretching pizza dough, and adding sauce and toppings like they were in some sort of race was fun. Plus, it was neat to see the ingredients they used. Her mouth was watering for one of those pizzas after just a few seconds.

'They have salads and pasta too.' Cole handed her a menu while a server delivered two ice waters. 'Get whatever you want.'

'I'll just have whatever you're having,' she said.

He frowned. 'I thought you could sort of practice being out —you know, ordering for yourself, things like that.'

Oh. So this wasn't just an enjoyable evening out — he was giving her a lesson. Teaching her how to be a normal person. She ducked her chin, suddenly ashamed that she thought she could just blend in with him, enjoy their time together. She was being scrutinized instead, and needed to earn his approval.

She opened her menu and began studying. Everything sounded delicious, but she knew she wanted to try one of those pizzas.

'Hi, have you guys been here before?' A bubbly server appeared in front of them.

'I have,' Cole said, 'but Savannah hasn't.'

'Oh, well welcome. Do you guys want to hear the specials, or do you already know what you want?' she asked, looking between them.

'Savannah?' Cole waited for her to answer.

'Um, I think I know what I want, but yes, I'd like to hear the specials.'

A smile tugged at the corner of Cole's mouth, seemingly pleased with Savannah's response. The waitress pulled out a notecard and read the specials. 'Okay, our chef's pizza tonight is fig and artichoke. The appetizer is a four-cheese grilled flatbread served with marinara sauce. What can I get for you?'

Savannah hesitated for a second. 'Get whatever you want,' Cole whispered, placing his hand on her knee.

His touch reassured her, even if it was a little distracting the way his large hand fit around her thigh. 'I'd like the vegetarian pizza with sausage, and a sweet tea, please.'

The waitress looked up from her pad. 'You want meat on a vegetarian pizza?'

'Yes. And I'd like an order of that four-cheese bread too.'

Cole chuckled under his breath. 'That sounds good. Make it two orders. Oh, and an Amstel please.'

After checking Cole's ID, the waitress scurried away. Cole removed his hand from her leg and draped it casually across the back of her seat.

'Did I do okay?' she asked, resisting the urge to nuzzle into his side.

'You did perfect.'

Savannah glowed at his compliment, fiddling with her napkin as she placed it across her lap.

Their drinks arrived and as she sipped her tea, Cole turned to study her, his brow furrowed like he was thinking hard about something. 'How are you feeling about staying with me?' He took a swig from his beer.

She thought of how to answer. Several words flitted through her mind. Safe. Relieved. But she said the first one that came to her lips. 'Happy.'

Cole continued watching her with a puzzled expression, but she couldn't tell if he was glad to hear that or not. A little bit of both, it seemed. 'How have things been going with Dr. White? Do you feel like you're making progress?'

She nodded. 'Yes, it's helping quite a bit. We're talking about things I haven't talked to anyone about before—things in my past. And we talk about my future, too.'

That word seemed to spark his curiosity. 'What do you want in your future, Savannah?'

She wanted what all women wanted: to belong, to be loved, to find a partner in life. Her therapist coaxed her into talking about her long buried feelings, and what she wanted. Now that she'd accepted it, the thoughts occupied a large section of her brain. And there was no separating those thoughts from thoughts of Cole. He'd stuck by her, taken care of her every need, and had never tried to take advantage. She knew better than to rely on someone she didn't know, but she'd been so helpless, so lost, she hadn't had a choice. And Cole had earned her trust and respect, something she didn't give out easily.

It was in this same conversation that Dr. White surprised her by asking if Cole had expressed a romantic interest in her, if he'd indicated he wanted something more than friendship. She'd said no. There had been nothing inappropriate in Cole's behavior towards her, and nothing that indicated he wanted more. But ever since that seed had been planted in her mind, she wondered why Cole hadn't. She studied her body in the mirror, wondering if she was attractive enough for him, and why he hadn't noticed her. She'd daydreamed about how he looked without his shirt. She was undeniably curious about his body, what it would be like to touch him, to have him touch her. She'd never been so interested in a man before, yet she couldn't deny her growing feelings for him.

Before Savannah could answer Cole's question, the waitress delivered their plates. The amount of food was way too much for two people. They would certainly be taking home leftovers, but Savannah enjoyed as much as she could until she was almost uncomfortably full.

After dinner, Cole walked her outside, tucking her inside his SUV. He leaned close and whispered. 'You still have to answer the question, Savannah.'

Her skin broke out in chill bumps and she merely nodded. The entire ride home she wondered if maybe—just maybe—he thought about the same things she did. The two of them together. Really together, not just stepping around each other in his condo. But neither of them spoke of the future for the rest of the night.

They watched TV on the couch until Savannah fell asleep. Cole carried her to bed, and just to see how far he'd let things go, she changed in his room, rather than her own. In the dimly lit room, she peeled off her jeans, then with her back to him she removed her sweater and bra. She could feel his eyes on her bare skin — her back, her bottom, clad in just the little white cotton panties he'd gotten for her. She could hear his breathing quicken and feel the electricity flowing between them. She wished she was brave enough to turn to him, to ask him to touch her, to kiss her, but of course she wasn't. She pulled one of his T-shirts over her head before turning to face him. His gaze was intense, burning into hers. His eyes travelled down from her face to her bare legs, the T-shirt hitting the tops of her thighs.

'Get covered up,' he said, his voice rough.

Savannah's first thought was that he was mad, until she realized the roughness in his voice, his burning gaze weren't due to anger, but desire. She barely contained a whimper at the realization, but did as he commanded and crawled into bed, pulling the sheet over her legs.

Cole joined her in bed. She reached for him, wanting to be closer, to tangle her legs with his, to hear him sooth her with gentle words like he did most nights, but he rolled away from her and whispered, 'Not tonight, Savannah.'

His words erected a wall between them, and though they shared a bed, she wondered if they'd ever share more.

Chapter 14

Saturday morning Marissa stormed past Cole without waiting for an invitation to enter the apartment. He'd been dodging her calls and avoiding her requests to come over for weeks — which was unusual. Typically where his sister was concerned, Cole did pretty much whatever she wanted.

'Where are they?' she asked sternly, brushing past him.

'Where are what?'

'The dead bodies.' She bypassed the kitchen, stepping down into the living room and looking around.

'The what?' Cole trailed after her, nervously glancing at the doorway to Savannah's room, where he was pretty sure she was hiding out.

'Or the prostitutes. Whatever it is you're hiding from me. God, I really should have encouraged you to date more. I worry about you, you know.'

He chuckled. 'Well, as you can see, there are no dead bodies — no prostitutes. Everything's fine, Rissa.' It was the nickname he given her when he was three and couldn't pronounce Marissa. And to her dismay, it had stuck for over twenty years.

A noise from the guest room grabbed her attention. 'What was that?'

Cole shifted uncomfortably and swore under his breath as Marissa started toward the room. He had no idea how to explain Savannah.

'Cole, did my timer go off?' Savannah emerged from the bedroom, wiping her hands on the apron fastened around her waist and headed for the kitchen. 'Oh. Hi.' She stopped suddenly, facing Marissa.

Marissa frowned, looking between Cole and Savannah and finally turned to him. 'Who is this?'

'This is…ah…' Cole stammered.

Savannah stepped forward, offering Marissa her hand. 'I'm Savannah. Cole's new cook.'

'Cook?' Marissa's face was full of doubt.

'Yes.' Savannah's gaze remained impassive. She didn't seem nearly as rattled as Cole felt. But he supposed it was at least in part true. Savannah was his cook… sort of. 'I take it you're his sister?' Savannah asked, wringing her hands in the apron.

Marissa nodded, watching Savannah curiously.

'Well, it's nice to meet you. If you'll excuse me I just need to take these scones from the oven.'

'You made scones?'

'Yes.'

'From scratch?' Marissa's eyebrows lifted.

'Of course.'

'I don't suppose I've ever had a homemade scone,' Marissa commented under her breath.

'Would you like one?'

'No, I wouldn't like one. I'd freakin' *love* one!'

Cole chuckled, watching the two women in the kitchen, Savannah removing the baking sheet from the oven while Marissa looked over her shoulder in astonishment at the lumpy scones. She was a sucker for baked goods just as much as he was.

Savannah served coffee and warm raspberry scones before scurrying off for her bedroom again. She might have shown courage in meeting Marissa, but Cole knew she wouldn't be comfortable engaging in small talk or answering questions about herself. Getting her to open up was a slow process.

Marissa's grin was as wide and suspicious as a damn Cheshire cat's. 'So she's your cook, huh?' She made a point of craning her neck to look down the hall and towards the bedroom where Savannah had disappeared. '*Live-in* cook?'

Cole managed not to spill his coffee, setting the mug down with shaky hands. 'Yeah, cook, and ah, housekeeper.'

Marissa broke off a small bite of the scone and popped it in her mouth. 'Oh my God. These are amazing.'

Cole relaxed into his seat. Savannah was an amazing cook, which lent a certain amount of credibility to their story.

'So is she why you've been hiding out?'

'I haven't been hiding, Marissa. Just busy is all.'

'Uh huh.'

Pulling something over on Marissa was near impossible. He knew from personal experience — she'd discovered his porn stash when he was fourteen, his pot when he was sixteen and of course both times she'd turned him in to their parents. She'd always been like a second mother to him, despite being only three years older.

They continued with small talk, Marissa complaining about her latest dating mishap — a blind date she'd met online who'd handed her his resume and the results of his recent physical on their first date. 'I swear I attract the strangest men.'

Cole grunted a response. He found that if he occasionally nodded in agreement, their conversations went smoother.

'Can I use your bathroom?'

Cole perked up. 'Ah, yeah, just use the one in my room. I'm not sure where Savannah is.'

'Kay.' Marissa sauntered off towards his room.

She was back a minute later, her face alight with playful suspicion. 'Cook and housekeeper huh?'

Cole's brow furrowed. 'What?'

'And that's why her panties are on the floor in your bathroom.'

Fuck. Cole had forgotten that she'd taken a bath in his Jacuzzi tub that morning. She'd left behind a tiny pair of pink panties lying on the bath mat, which he'd stood and stared at for a good ten minutes, unsure what to do with. He'd ultimately left them there, thinking maybe she'd come back for them.

Cole stalked from the room, grabbing the panties from where they lay on the floor and stuffed them into the bathroom drawer. Dammit. He would not have Marissa making a big deal about this. He didn't want Savannah embarrassed, or worse, ashamed. She hadn't done anything wrong. But he knew that sooner or later, Marissa would figure out the truth – well maybe not the actual truth – that Savannah was a refugee from the cult, but most likely she'd come to the conclusion that they were dating and then pepper Savannah with questions. He couldn't let that happen.

Returning to the living room, he pulled Marissa aside. 'Listen. She's not my cook, or my housekeeper.'

Her mouth curled into a grin. 'No shit. Well it's about freaking time you started dating someone! How am I ever going to be an auntie if you don't find a girl? I mean, I want kids of my own, but you know the next best thing would be…'

'Stop.' Cole held a hand up. 'She's not my girlfriend, either. Savannah's only nineteen.'

Marissa's hands flew to her hips. 'Damn. A little young, don't you think? And if you haven't forgotten, your date with my friend Sali is next weekend. I want to make sure you're not involved with another woman. Girl. Whatever.'

'Listen, I'll explain everything to you, but I need you to trust me.'

Her gaze softened. 'I do trust you, Colby. You know that.'

He nodded. 'Then come sit down.' He led her to the sofa and settled in across from her.

Thankfully, he didn't have to worry about Savannah over-hearing, because just then she emerged from her room, saying she needed to take Cuddles outside. Marissa, of course, had to meet Cuddles, which resulted in lots of baby talk and snuggling the little beast. Cole made himself scarce, pouring them another cup of coffee and grabbing more scones.

Once Savannah was outside, Cole explained the whole story about finding Savannah at the compound, rescuing her from that crappy halfway house and that she'd been living with him for three weeks in secret. He knew the Bureau would freak if they knew, but he didn't have it in him to send her away. He left out the part about Savannah invading his brain at pretty much every waking hour, making it hard to concentrate at work, the gym, and especially at home.

Marissa remained silent while he spoke, nodding and looking concerned. 'Wow. That's quite a story. Tell me the truth, Cole, are you two… lovers?' She swallowed roughly.

Cole knew the wrong answer would earn him a thump upside the head, but he answered truthfully —that he hadn't so much as touched her. Not sexually at least.

'Good. She's too young for you.'

'And too damaged,' Cole pointed out. 'She sees a therapist though and seems to be doing better.'

'And the dog?'

'Her therapist's idea. Animal therapy or something like that.'

'Hmpf.' Marissa nodded. 'Are you sure you know what you're doing Colby?'

'Yes.' *No.*

'Well don't forget about the date with Sali. You're still going, right?'

'Course.' *Crap.* He'd hoped to get out of that. 'I'll go on the date—*if* you'll do me a favor.' Cole turned on his best *pretty please for your little brother* smile. 'Take Savannah shopping?' He fished his credit card from his pocket and handed it to her. 'She needs clothes, shoes—she needs pretty much everything.'

She jerked the card from his hand with a grin. 'Now that I can do.'

Savanna returned a few minutes later with Cuddles nestled in her arms like she was the damn thing's personal throne. He resisted the urge to roll his eyes, and eased the dog out of her grasp. 'I'll watch Cuddles. I want you to go with Marissa to buy some new clothes, and whatever else you need, okay?'

She studied his expression for just a second before her face broke out in a huge grin. 'Okay.' She lifted on her toes and planted a kiss to his cheek. 'Thank you.'

'Go on now,' he managed.

Once Savannah and Marissa were gone Cole was drawn like a magnet back into his master bath. He pulled open the drawer containing Savannah's panties and stared down at the small piece of illicit fabric. Pale pink lace panties. He would have taken Savannah for more of a white cotton briefs kind of girl. He held them up to inspect. They were high cut, likely showing off generous portions of her perfect ass. *Da-mn.* He tossed the panties onto the vanity and turned on the shower.

As steamy vapors lazily drifted toward the ceiling, he couldn't resist any longer. He brought the panties to his nose and inhaled the pungent feminine aroma. His cock jumped at the scent. He'd been fantasizing about Savannah for far too long and if he didn't get some relief soon he was going to combust.

With one hand still clutching the panties, his other worked to free himself from the confines of his jeans. He was already rock hard, his dick swollen and ready. He stroked himself hard and fast, pumping without mercy as Savannah's scent filled his senses. His long measured strokes turned harder, uneven, as his thoughts turned towards Savannah. Her soft skin, her preference to be held in his arms, and the light feminine scent of her skin. He pumped faster, praying for relief to come. His legs trembled, and he reached one hand to the counter to support his weight just as his orgasm hit.

Chapter 15

Cole and his older sister shared a resemblance in their coloring—both had dark hair and inquisitive, yet kind, mocha-colored eyes. But the similarities ended there. Whereas Cole was the strong, silent type, Marissa was talkative and outgoing.

On the way there, she overwhelmed Savannah with questions and, unused to talking about herself so much, Savannah struggled to keep up as they moved through topics ranging from her upbringing to her future plans.

Yes, she liked living with Cole.

Yes, she missed the compound, but only because of all the little ones. There was always something that needed doing and she liked feeling useful.

No, she'd never dated.

No, nothing was going on between her and Cole.

Why did everyone keep asking her that? And why did they seem surprised when she said nothing was? Perhaps they thought like Jacob, that a man's only interest in her was physical, but so far Cole had given her no indication that was the case.

Marissa misread her silence. 'It's okay, you can trust Cole.'

Savannah merely nodded. Somehow she knew that.

A few minutes later, Marissa parked in the mall's overflow lot, and then turned to look at Savannah. 'You ready to do some damage?' she smiled.

'Sure.'

They set off for the entrance, Savannah hesitating at the automatic gliding doors. Marissa stopped at her side.

'Are you okay? Being in public like this?'

Savannah nodded, though she supposed it was a fair question, this was a new experience for her. One of many lately. 'Are you kidding, I've dreamt of this moment.'

Savannah dutifully followed Marissa into at least a dozen different stores, accepted armfuls of clothes, modeled the garments in the fitting room, and graciously waited while Marissa looked her over, commenting on what worked, and what didn't. When they made their way up to the register, Marissa piled the clothes onto the counter and handed over Cole's credit card.

Savannah snatched back a few of the garments. 'It's okay. I don't need all of these. Just because they fit doesn't mean I should get all of them.'

Marissa took the items from her and handed them back to the cashier, frowning at Savannah.

'Marissa,' Savannah pleaded. 'This is too much. I can't let Cole pay for all this.' She would never be able to pay Cole back at this rate.

Marissa rolled her eyes. 'Oh yes you can. And you will. That boy's got more money than he knows what to do with. Every week he stuffs his paycheck in the bank for savings. Besides, he told me to make sure you get everything you need. If I bring you back with one little bag of stuff, he'll be pissed. Trust me.'

Savannah couldn't really imagine Cole being pissed off, but she trusted Marissa, and she didn't want to be responsible for making him angry. Especially since he had done so much for her already. She nodded her head in acquiescence.

But Savannah did draw the line at getting herself one of the gorgeous handbags she noticed in the department store they went to. She didn't *need* it. So it felt wrong to indulge at Cole's expense, despite Marissa's urgings.

Several pairs of jeans later, more than a dozen tops, three pairs of shoes, an assortment of bras and panties, and even a little bit of makeup, Savannah was exhausted. They stopped for lunch at Marissa's favorite Mexican restaurant, where she had her first ever burrito, a delicious vegetarian concoction. She made a mental note to prepare for Cole at home sometime.

'This is it? This is all you got?' Cole pursued the half-dozen shopping bags littering the entryway to his condo.

'Told you.' Marissa shot a satisfied look at Savannah.

Savannah walked over to Cole and hugged her arms around his waist, sucking the breath from his lungs, more out of surprise than anything else. 'Thank you.'

'You're welcome.' He patted her back carefully while Marissa scrutinized them.

Savannah shuffled off to her room, toting several of the bags.

'You guys got a chance to talk?' Cole asked his sister.

Marissa nodded, handing him the last of the shopping bags. 'Yes, she's a really nice girl. Despite her upbringing, she's surprisingly normal. She's got a good head on her shoulders.'

He agreed, peeking into a pink bag filled with panties. Whoa. His eyes shot back up to Marissa's, hoping his desire wasn't reflected in his eyes. 'Yeah, thanks for taking her out.'

Savannah returned, carrying Cuddles on her hip. 'Thanks for today. Both of you.' Savannah smiled.

'Oh! And guess what?' Marissa asked, looking at Cole. 'We ran into Levi outside and guess what? Savannah is going on her very first date!' Marissa squealed.

Savannah's eyes nervously darted to Cole's, as if bracing for his response.

Damn meddling Marissa had gone too far this time. Way too fucking far. 'No,' he barked out. He turned to stalk off for his bedroom.

He heard Marissa tell Savannah that she'd fix this and she trailed after him down the hall. Cole didn't bother to lock his bedroom door, knowing Marissa would beat on it and demand to be let in, or carry on the conversation through the door, probably loud enough that the neighbors would hear.

He heard the door open as she slipped in behind him, but Cole remained facing the window, looking down on the traffic below. He didn't even want to think about Savannah dating. 'She's not ready for that, Rissa. You need to stop interfering. Not everyone wants to fucking date all the damn time. Just because you're over thirty and single, and miserable being alone, doesn't mean everyone else is too. Christ…' He ran his hands through his hair, pulling it in opposing angles and released a heavy sigh.

When he turned and faced Marissa, his expression softened. Damn, her lip was trembling.

'I was trying to help. Savannah's nineteen going on twenty soon, Cole. She wants to date. She wants to be normal. She told me that herself.'

'She wants to date?'

'Yes. Maybe it's time you stopped treating her like she's some sick little kid, and let her spread her wings a little. She's young and she's been hurt, but she's not stupid.'

Fuck. Marissa had spent one afternoon with Savannah and had already gotten more out of her than he had. He looked at Marissa and saw the hurt in her eyes . She'd only been trying to help, and he'd snapped at her. 'Hey, I'm sorry about what I said. You know that any guy would be lucky to have you.'

Marissa took a deep breath and squared her shoulders. 'This isn't about me. Tell me why you reacted like that to Savannah going out on a date.'

'I don't know.'

She stepped in closer to him. 'I think you do. Is it because you don't like the idea of another guy with Savannah?'

Cole scrubbed a hand across his jaw. 'I don't want him pawing all over her. She wouldn't know what to do, how to protect herself.'

'Cole,' she scolded. 'She's an adult. She can handle herself. But if you're so worried, go with them.'

Ha laughed. 'Like a chaperone?'

'No, you idiot.' She swatted his shoulder. 'Isn't Levi's mom that cougar who wants you?'

He nodded. There was no denying the woman had been after him since he moved in three years ago.

'So make it a double date. You and the cougar, and Levi and Savannah. It'll be good practice for her — something normal that she can do, and you'll be close by in case he gets grabby.'

He smiled at his sister. 'And who's going to protect me when the cougar gets too grabby with me?'

She laughed. 'I have a feeling you can handle yourself. Besides, maybe you'll even have fun.'

He supposed it could work. There was just one little problem. He didn't like the idea of anyone other than him taking Savannah on her first date. At least he'd be there for it. A compromise he supposed he could live with.

Chapter 16

Cole and Savannah were enjoying a lazy Saturday afternoon when a loud buzzing from the intercom system grabbed their attention. 'Are you expecting someone?' Savannah asked.

Cole shook his head. He didn't like the idea of anyone interrupting the private bubble he and Savannah had created the past several weeks. He punched the button on the wall. 'Yeah?'

Static crackled through the speaker. 'Uh, yes, my name is Dillon James. I'm looking for Savannah.'

Cole whipped around to face Savannah. Her face had gone pale and her hands were shaking. She slowly shook her head, bringing her finger to her lips.

How the hell had Dillon tracked Savannah here? Cole gave a tight nod and pressed the talk button to reply. 'Sorry, no one named Savannah lives here.'

It took everything in him not to go rushing down the stairs and into the lobby to face this asshole. He turned to Savannah instead. 'You okay?'

Her eyes remained locked on his, full of intensity.

'He can't hear us, Savannah.'

She drew a shaky breath. 'I just…it's probably stupid of me, I just don't want to see him right now. He won't like me living here with you. I don't want to deal with him.'

Cole went to her side, placing a hand on her shoulder. 'It's not stupid. You don't have to face him. You're safe here. Okay?' Her shoulders shook and his hand automatically rubbed out the tension. It didn't escape his notice that Savannah was in a near panic at both seeing Dillon and fear that he'd snap seeing Savannah with another man. The thought did not sit well with him. He hadn't been in a proper fist fight over a girl since sixth grade, but he wouldn't hesitate now if the occasion called.

She nodded. 'Thank you, Cole. For everything.'

Cole folded her into his arms, unsure of how to comfort her. He hated that Savannah had a history with that creep, and that she had grown up around men with screwed up belief systems. He wished he could shield her from it all, but he'd settle for holding her, and for her part, Savannah clung to him like he was the last tree standing in a thunderstorm. It broke his heart, and renewed his decision to protect her all at once.

That evening, as Cole dressed in dark jeans and a light blue button down shirt, he knew he needed to tell Savannah about his date with Sali. He sprayed a squirt of his seldom-worn cologne onto his neck, and ran his hands through his hair in an attempt to tame it. He hadn't thought much of going out with the girl when Marissa approached him about the idea. And even though only a few weeks had passed since he agreed to the date, somehow he felt closer to Savannah. Perhaps it was seeing her with Levi, or that he no longer fought off her cuddling at night, or because the other night felt like a date between them, but whatever the reason, he felt strange telling her.

He found her in the living room, her knees drawn to her chest on the couch. 'Hey Savannah.' She turned to face him, cradling Cuddles in her arms. 'I'll be going out later. You don't need to cook dinner tonight.' He wondered what Savannah would make of him going on a date . And if he was going to have the balls to tell her.

'Oh. Okay. I can eat some of the leftover pizza from last night. And Cuddles and I will probably just watch a movie.'

'Okay. Remember to keep the door locked.'

'I will,' she promised. 'Cole?'

'Yes?'

'Where are you going?'

He hesitated only a second. He wouldn't lie to Savannah. Besides he was free to go on dates. 'My sister set me up on a blind date.'

'Oh.' Her bottom lip jutted out just slightly. 'But I'll see you later, when you get home?'

'Yes,' he reassured her. 'I'll be back later tonight.'

It remained unspoken between them, but both knew they'd be sleeping together in his bed later.

He set off to meet Sali at the pub. He'd have preferred to pick her up, but as Marissa reminded him, girls don't let men they don't know pick them up. He could be some creepy stalker, and then he'd have her address. He assured her he wasn't going to begin stalking her friend from yoga, but that had only started Marissa on a whole other rant that he obviously didn't date enough if he didn't know the simplest of rules.

When Cole entered the pub he searched out Liam first. A lot of times he could be found behind the bar, providing a second set of hands for the bartender rather than sit alone in his office in the back. And tonight proved no different. Liam nodded once, spotting Cole across the room. Liam was his last single friend, but he certainly didn't lack for female companionship being the owner of a popular bar. It was meeting quality girls that he found difficult. Cole knew that if Liam met the right girl, he wouldn't be opposed to settling down. He and Liam had been friends for over twenty years. In college, they had often tricked girls into thinking they were brothers. They were both a few inches over six feet, with dark hair and when neither had shaved for a few days, which Liam often neglected to do, they took on an uncanny resemblance.

Cole took a frustrated breath. He wasn't sure how he was going to find her. He saw two single women at either end of the bar. One was a knockout blonde, beautiful with legs up to her tits. His sister didn't love him that much. The other woman was plain brunette, a few pounds overweight and glasses so big, they belonged in another decade. He shook his head, wondering if he could just slip out before she noticed him. Damn Marissa. She'd roped him into shit like this before, always using the phrase, '*Well I thought she was cute*,' to clear her conscience.

He took a deep breath. One drink. He could do this. One stiff as fuck drink. He took one last wistful look at the gorgeous blonde and approached the brunette instead. 'Hi, you must be Sali.'

Her face pinched in confusion. 'No, sorry.'

His head swung around and he met the blonde's eyes as a slow grin spread across his face. Marissa loved him after all.

He left the brunette staring after him and approached the blonde. 'Please tell me you're Sali.'

She smiled. 'Cole, I presume?'

Dear God, she had an Australian accent. His sister *really* loved him.

He slid in next to her and they each ordered a drink. Sali knew his sister from yoga, but Marissa hadn't mentioned that Sali was the instructor. They shared some laughs about Marissa's clumsy mishaps in yoga, talked about where she grew up in Australia, and he made her laugh with his poor attempt at an Aussie accent.

One drink turned into two, and then three. She was easygoing, flirty and sexy as hell. That accent had him half hard all night. At first he felt guilty about leaving Savannah alone, but as the alcohol softened his mood, he figured perhaps some time apart may do them both good. She needed to gain some independence from him, and Lord knew he needed to get her off his mind.

When Sali excused herself for the restroom, Cole took stock of how the night was going. They were getting along well, and she'd begun leaning in towards him, placing her hand on his thigh as she laughed, or finding other ways to brush up against him, like pressing her breast into his arm when she reached across the bar for her drink. Cole wondered if she'd be game for continuing things back at her place.

Sali returned with a fresh coat of pink gloss on her lips and a seductive smile. Finding that his patience and manners had disappeared along with that last drink, Cole stood and pulled her against him. 'Let's go somewhere,' he whispered low, near her ear.

She smiled a little, her eyes dancing on his. 'What did you have in mind?' A playful smirk tugged on her mouth.

'Somewhere we can be alone.' Without waiting for her to answer, Cole took her hand and pulled her outside of the club. They waited on the sidewalk, Sali's arms wrapped around his middle.

'And here I thought you were a nice guy. Your sister had you pegged to be some saint. I thought tonight was going to be totally dull.'

'It doesn't have to be.' He leaned over and pressed a soft kiss on her mouth, testing her. She wrapped her hands around his neck, pulling him even closer. Fuck he needed this, needed the distraction before he did something with Savannah he'd regret.

'I have roommates. We can't go my place,' she whispered.

'It's okay, we'll be quiet,' he said between kisses. Well he would, he couldn't say the same for her, since he was hoping to make her scream.

She pressed a hand against his chest. 'I can't, sexy. I share a room with Jenny. She'll kill me if I bring a guy home again.'

Again? He wondered how often she did this, but let it go. Cole supposed he had a roommate too, though he had no idea how to explain Savannah.

'Let's go to your place,' Sali suggested, placing a hand over the already hard budge in his jeans and gave him a squeeze.

Cole reluctantly agreed. Well, not all that reluctantly. The thought of getting laid and pushing Savannah into the back corner of his mind, if only for thirty minutes or so, sounded too good to pass up. He only hopped Savannah wasn't in his bed. He'd do a sweep of the apartment first, and hell if necessary, he'd fuck Sali in his truck.

Cole realized he was in no shape to drive. 'Okay, come on We'll grab a cab.'

Sali spent the ride in the cab licking his neck and gripping the hard ridge in his jeans. He knew he had a freaky girl on his hands. The thought made him both deliriously happy and nervous since the last thing he wanted to do was hurt Savannah. He warned Sali that he had someone staying with him right now, and they'd have to be extra quiet. In between nibbling on his earlobe, and licking his neck, she said no problem.

They staggered from the cab into the stairwell, kissing and groping each other as they went.

'Remember, extra quiet,' he reminded her when he unlocked the door.

Rather than answering, Sali worked her hand into the front of his jeans and gave him a gentle squeeze. He closed his eyes, imaging briefly it was Savannah's hand around him. His eyes shot open. Where had that thought come from? He would never be with Savannah. Not like this. He pulled Sali's hand from his pants and asked her to wait in the kitchen.

The living room was empty, which meant Savannah was in bed — but he had no idea if that meant his bed or hers. The door to the guest room was closed. He continued past it and into his own bedroom. It was empty. He breathed a little sigh of relief. God, he was so on edge about Savannah finding out about this, he wondered if he should just usher Sali out before this blew up in his face. But when he turned, Sali was already standing on the threshold of his bedroom.

'Weren't going to get started without me, were you?' She grinned and stalked towards him.

He swallowed and watched her lean, lithe body cross the room. He'd be lying if he said he didn't want this. His dick was already straining against his jeans, only he didn't know if it was because of the thought of Savannah discovering them or because of Sali's long legs wrapped around his waist.

She closed the door behind her, flipped off the lights and shoved him down onto the bed. His back hit the mattress with a thud. Sali straddled him and pulled off her shirt. Maybe he could just make this quick and get her out of the apartment. Cole moved through the foreplay faster than he liked to. 'Are you ready for me?' he asked, nuzzling her neck with kisses.

He usually liked to make sure the girl got off at least once, and was nice and wet before he sunk into her. But something told him Sali wouldn't mind moving onto the main event. She pulled her panties aside and pleasured herself while he watched, then brought her fingers to his mouth. He opened obediently. 'See I'm already wet,' she whispered.

Good. Let's get on with it. Listening to his inner dialogue was like having an angel on one shoulder, a devil on the other. Half of him wanted to fuck her senseless, to lose himself in the pleasure, and the other half wished he'd never brought her home so he could be curled up next to Savannah. But God, it wasn't like he and Savannah were in a relationship. He should be dating other women. But sleeping with them in the apartment he shared with Savannah? That part was questionable.

Cole grabbed a condom from the drawer in his nightstand and handed it to Sali. 'Put it on me,' he growled.

Sali obliged, tearing the package open with her teeth, and planting a kiss on the head of his dick before rolling the condom down to the base of his shaft. He picked her up under her arms and lifted her on top of him so she was straddling his lap. Then he folded his arms behind his head and grinned up at her in a challenging smirk. He had a feeling he could bend her into a pretzel, with her being a yoga instructor and all, but somehow the idea held no appeal. He could tell that Sali was the type of girl who liked to be in charge, who'd be happy to ride him until they both came.

She lowered herself down slowly on his shaft, throwing her head back in ecstasy as he disappeared inside her. Sali increased her speed, alternating between rolling her hips and bouncing against him. She let out little breathy moans and grunts each time he hit the right spot. As her speed increased, so did her volume. 'Yeah… rightthere…rightthere…' she moaned.

Cole planted his palm across her mouth. 'Shh.' He kept his hand secured across her lips as she moved against him. She was oblivious to his hand, and continued riding him.

After a few minutes, Cole opened to eyes to see if Sali was getting closer to finishing. He sure as hell wasn't. He didn't know why, but something felt off. He just couldn't get into it. Cole noticed the room wasn't quite as dark as it was before, and his eyes flashed around Sali's writhing form to his bedroom door, which was now partially opened. How the hell had that happened? Light from the hallway flooded the entrance to his room. Lifting his head from the pillow, he saw Savannah standing in the doorway watching them.

Holy shit.

Her eyes were locked on his, blazing with curiosity. His dick jerked inside Sali.

'Oh yeah. Just like that,' she moaned. He clamped his hand tighter over her mouth. Sali was completely in her own world, not even noticing that they weren't alone, or that all of Cole's attention was on Savannah.

Savannah's gaze flickered to Sali's back, her ass lifting up and down on Cole.

Savannah was dressed in just a pair of panties and a tank top. She looked so innocent, yet completely fucking sexy, it made him even harder. Her lips were parted, pulling in shallow breaths and her eyes were dark with desire.

Savannah just stood watching them for several minutes, her eyes never wavering from his, until Sali gave a little shout and then climbed off of him. Savannah turned and ran for her bedroom.

'Did you finish?' Sali asked.

'Yeah,' he choked out. He doubted she'd check the condom for evidence. He peeled it off and wrapped it in tissue, hoping to keep up the ruse that it was full, and threw it in the waste basket beside his bed. There was no way he was going to be able to come with Sali. Unless he replaced the image of Sali with Savannah, but God he couldn't think like that. It wasn't right.

'Hey, I hope you don't mind.' Sali threw her top on over her head. 'But I don't like to stick around after, so I already texted my roommate to come get me and she's here.' She held up her phone, the flashing blue light indicating a new message.

Cole didn't plan on trying to talk her into staying. 'Yeah okay. Well, thanks.'

'No problem, sexy. That was fun, yeah?' Sali slipped on the rest of her clothes, while Cole stepped into a pair of jeans.

After seeing Sali out, Cole stood in the dark entryway completely bewildered and out of sorts. He cursed and fought the urge to punch the wall. He caught his reflection in the hallway mirror, and the pale, haunted man staring back at him was almost unrecognizable. He didn't know why he had thought it had been okay to bring Sali home, because it most certainly was not fucking okay. Not at all. He had sobered up the instant Savannah's eyes met his.

He took a deep breath and approached her bedroom door, which was left cracked open. He found Savannah sitting in the center of her bed, still dressed in just a pair of panties and white tank. Her gaze was cast down, and the sadness in her pose, the limp slump of her shoulders hit him like a physical pain in the chest. 'Savannah.' His voice broke and the ache in his chest made it difficult to breathe. Not getting any response from her, he approached the bed.

Savannah's eyes followed his feet across the carpet, until he was standing at the end of her bed. She looked up at him, chewing on her bottom lip. She watched him like he was some wild creature. Her lips were parted, her eyes wide, and her breathing shallow.

'Are you okay?' he asked.

Wide green eyes studied his. She nodded slowly. Her gaze lowered, lingering across his bare chest and stomach and stopping at the waist band of his jeans, which he'd left unbuttoned in his haste to get Sali out the door.

Her hands toyed with the edge of her tank top, and Cole's lungs tightened. *What was she...* She lifted the top, exposing the soft skin of her belly and continued raising it slowly until her breasts came into view. Cole couldn't help but follow her movements. He bit his lip and looked down at her. Soft milky skin and pale pink nipples, tightening in the cool air. Fuck, she was perfect, better than his imagination. He swallowed roughly.

'You can't do that, Savannah.' He reached for the discarded shirt and handed it back to her.

She accepted the shirt from him, only to throw it across the room. Damn, she was severely overestimating his self-control. He'd give his next breath just to taste her beautiful tits.

'Savannah,' he ground out through clenched teeth. 'Get dressed.' His command sounded weak even to his own ears.

She sucked her lip into her mouth rolled over with a huff, lying on her stomach and burying her face in the pillow.

Why did she seem hurt? He curled his hands into fists, then straightened them and sat next to her on the bed.

Her fine little ass was on full display in the barely there pink panties that made appearances in his dreams. His breath caught as he took in the sight of the shapely, round globes of her ass, just begging for his attention.

He placed his hand on her bare back, rubbing the skin between her shoulder blades with his thumb. She turned her head to the side, resting one cheek against the pillow so she could look up at him. 'I'm sorry you had to see that. I shouldn't have brought her home.'

'Then why did you?' she challenged.

Because he'd been thinking with his dick. But he couldn't say that to Savannah, so he didn't say anything, and she didn't press him. He continued running his palm along her back.

'Are you going to do that to me — what you did to her?' she asked.

'No,' his voice came out impossibly tight. 'You're safe with me, Savannah. I won't hurt you.'

She chewed on her lip. 'It didn't look like you were hurting her.' She batted her eyelashes.

'Savannah stop,' he pleaded.

'Unless she was hurting you...' her brow creased. He remembered the way Sali had ridden him — hard and fast, just the balls of her feet on the bed, her hands pressed onto his pecs as she bounced against him.

'No,' he choked out. God, she really didn't know anything about sex.

He couldn't resist running his fingertips down her back, over her spine and up to her neck again. It was a touch meant to sooth her, so why the hell was it turning him on?

He wanted to ask why she'd watched them, but held back, not sure he could handle the answer. 'Savannah? Tell me what's wrong,' he coaxed, carefully rubbing her bare back, but she remained still and quiet. He trailed his fingertips up to her shoulders, then back down to where her lower back dipped in. He let his hands venture farther, just to the edge of her panties, before sweeping his fingers up her spine again. He felt her breathing shallow out and grow faster.

God, how badly he wanted to touch her ass. To grip it in his palms and maybe even rain little smacks across it. She had a perfect ass, after all.

He continued massaging her back, and felt her slowly begin to relax into the mattress. But then she did something she shouldn't have. She moaned and wiggled that little ass as she got more comfortable. Damn. Unable to resist her any longer, Cole brought both hands to her backside and cupped it in his palms needing to touch, to massage every part of her. Savannah let out another breathy moan and he thought his heart stopped. She lifted her bottom just slightly, as if to meet his hands. The skin was so soft, so smooth, and tempting as fuck. He wanted to pull her panties down and touch her bare ass, but he didn't dare. Instead he continued rubbing her back, and letting his hands spend more and more time squeezing and cupping her ass as his hands wandered lower. Savannah's breathing had quickened and she turned her head, no longer burying it in the pillow so she could fully watch him. The agony in her expression had disappeared and was replaced by desire and that burning curiosity he'd seen when she'd watched him with Sali.

'Cole,' she whispered.

Somehow he knew it wasn't a command to stop, but an encour-agement to go farther. He knew he shouldn't, but fuck, he was so turned on. Just a little farther, he wouldn't let himself do anything he shouldn't, but he so badly wanted to taste her sweet skin, and feel her writhe against his mouth. He trailed his hands down the backs of her thighs, tickling the sensitive skin behind her knees, and when he brought both hands up over her ass, he let his fingers slip just inside the elastic so he could feel her bare skin, uninterrupted by the fabric. It was as far as he'd go without some signal from her that she wanted more. He continued kneading and massaging her plump flesh, his fingers working closer and closer to her little pussy. He wanted to know if she was wet, because he was hard as a rock and she hadn't even touched him yet. She wouldn't even need to touch him; he could probably come just thinking about her ass.

Savannah's breathing became more erratic, and she lifted her hips just slightly, as if giving his hands better access to touch her down below, if he wanted to. With both hands now under the fabric of her panties, he bent and kissed the back of one thigh, then the other, planting open-mouthed kisses along her tender flesh. When his tongue lavished the skin at the back of her knee, her hips shot of the bed.

'Ah,' she gasped.

'Shh, I'll make it better,' he promised. He kissed his way up her legs, and rained tender kisses over her backside, fighting the urge to nuzzle his face in between her cheeks. He didn't want to scare her, but he did love her ass. With one hand pushing aside the fabric of her panties, his other found her slick heat. Fuck, she was soaking wet. His dick twitched against the confines of his jeans.

Savannah pushed back against his hand. He reveled in the soft feel of her little pussy, her plump lips, and the slick heat emanating from her. He swirled one finger at her opening, gathering the moisture he found there and swept his finger over the little swollen bud.

'Cole!' Savannah's voice was insistent and sure. He knew he couldn't leave her like this, he wanted to make her come more than he wanted his next breath. He slid her panties down her legs, still leaving her lying on her stomach so her ass was on display. His hands massaged the silken flesh, gripping her cheeks and spreading them so he could see the delicate pink puckered flesh there and then further down, to the slick dampness between her legs. It was insanely hot. His dick was harder than it'd ever been. His thumbs brushed against her backside, drawing over the tender flesh at her center and Savannah's breathing hitched. He placed a kiss on her lower back and then urged her to roll over.

She lay facing him against the pillow, her breasts rising and falling with each ragged breath she drew.

She was perfect. Her skin was taunt across her stomach and hips, her tits perky with pink nipples that were begging to be licked. He placed a sweet, damp kiss against her cheek, just at the corner of her mouth, and then moved down, nibbling the tender flesh of her neck, planting kisses along her collarbone, over her heart, before kissing each breast. His tongue lavished attention on her swollen nipples, suckling each one deep into his mouth while his tongue flicked back and forth. Savannah moaned loudly and thrashed against the pillow.

He shifted so he was lying beside her, his face level with her belly. With his eyes on hers, he parted her legs, and lowered his mouth to taste her. Savannah's head dropped back to the pillow and her eyes rolled closed. He was too turned on to go slow and flicked his tongue ruthlessly against her, sucking her into his mouth until she was moaning, and writhing and calling his name. A few seconds later, he felt when she came, her little pussy spasming like it was clutching for something to fill it. But that would not be happening. He'd ice down his dick if he had to. Savannah wasn't ready, and besides he wasn't meant to be her first.

He kissed her thighs and belly until the aftershocks of her orgasm subsided, and then shifted on the bed to sit next to her.

'Colby…' she moaned. 'I'm dizzy.' She clutched at the bed sheets, attempting to ground herself.

He smiled as pride swelled inside him. That must have been one powerful orgasm. He smoothed her hair back from her face, enjoying the look of bliss he put there.

She looked up at him with cloudy unfocused eyes. 'Make the room stop spinning…' she groaned.

Wait a second… His stomach dropped. *What the fuck?* 'Are you drunk?'

She let out a giggle. 'Just a little.'

'Christ, Savannah.' He stood, and pulled her panties up her legs. This sooo should not have happened. Cole stepped away from her on shaky legs and adjusted the huge erection tugging against his zipper. Her wide eyes followed his movements. A twinge of disappointment colored her features, but Cole ignored it. He stalked out to the kitchen and found a bottle of vodka and the orange juice sitting on the island. Savannah had broken into his liquor cabinet like a damn rebellious teenager. Is this what her therapist had warned him about? She'd gotten drunk, and apparently horny, and he'd fallen for it, hook, line and sinker.

With the scent of her still clinging to his lips and fingers, Cole fled to the master bathroom. He dragged his jeans down just enough to free his erection and pumped a squirt of hand lotion into his palm. He rubbed it against his cock, pumping and thrusting his hips in time to match his hand's frenzied movements. Only a few strokes later, he came with a breathy moan, emptying himself into the palm of his other hand.

After washing up, he returned to his bedroom and found Savannah sitting in the center of his bed.

Their eyes locked on each other's, and he read hers for signs that she regretted what they'd done moments ago, but found none.

'It smells like her in here.' Savannah wrinkled her nose.

Cole began working to change the sheets and pillow cases. If she wasn't going to bring up what he'd just done to her, neither was he. He gathered a clean set of sheets and tossed them on the mattress. He wouldn't make Savannah sleep where he'd just bed another woman, but he also wouldn't turn her away now. She'd been too vulnerable, let her guard down with him completely. And if this is where she wanted to be, he wouldn't deny her. Couldn't. Not now. Maybe not ever.

'Cole?' Her voice had a pleading quality, like she needed reassurance about where they now stood.

'Get in bed, Savannah.'

She turned for the door. His hand on her elbow stopped her. 'No, in my bed. With me.'

She smiled and crawled in beside him, laying her head on his chest once they were settled in the darkness.

'I don't want you drinking, Savannah.'

'I, I'm sorry. Are you mad at me?'

'No, I'm not mad at you.' Mad at himself was more like it. He shouldn't have touched her. But now that he had, he wanted nothing more than to do it again and again. 'Are you still drunk?'

'I'm not drunk. I only had a little bit while I waited for you to get home. I just wanted to see what it was like.'

He couldn't be upset with Savannah. He'd left her alone tonight to go out with another woman. Savannah had gotten bored. She'd done what a lot of nineteen-almost-twenty-year-olds did on the weekends.

'How are you feeling now?' he asked, needing some indication of what was going on inside her head.

'Fine.'

'Just fine?' He smirked, turning to look at her.

She smiled against his skin, then yawned. 'I'm sleepy. You stayed out late.'

He didn't point out that she was most likely drained from the combination of the alcohol and the powerful orgasm he'd given her, rather than the late hour. 'Was that okay, what happened in your room?'

'Yes. It's just…'

'Just what?' he prompted, his heart kicking up speed. He didn't want to hear her say she regretted it. He sure as hell didn't.

'You didn't kiss me. And you didn't let me touch you.'

'You wanted that?'

She nodded, her face still turned down.

'Are you a virgin?' he whispered.

The muscles in her back tensed, and his hand stilled against her skin.

'Yes.'

Relief flooded his system. 'Good. You're going to stay that way.'

'But Cole…'

'No. Don't say anything else right now. We're not talking about that. Especially not when you've been drinking.'

She let out a deep sigh. 'Can I just say one thing?'

He clenched his fist at his side, knowing it'd be futile to refuse her request. 'One.'

She took a deep breath as if preparing to give a speech. 'When I'm with Dr. White, or Marissa, they see me as a normal girl, with normal wants and needs — to be loved, to have physical affection—but sometimes I don't think you see me like that. You still look at me like I'm the scared, crying girl you pulled out of that compound. I just want you to know — I want more.'

He took a second to let her words sink in. It had only been a few weeks. Did she really know what she wanted? Was she even capable of more right now? He didn't want to think about her dating. In fact, the idea scared the shit out of him. But she was a bright, pretty girl. He couldn't just keep her hidden away, no matter how much he might want to. Perhaps the alcohol had loosened her tongue some, but it was true, she didn't sound drunk. Not at all. She sounded confident and sure. 'That's good Savannah. I want you to have those things too. You deserve all of that and more.' But he knew he was not the man for her. He could come up with a list of a thousand reasons why: he was too old for her; she needed more time to heal; he was married to his job; he wasn't looking for a relationship; and the list went on and on. But tell that to his body. He wanted her, even though he knew it was impossible.

'Savannah?' he whispered in the darkness, unable to stop himself from following up on her comment about kissing him.

'Yes?'

'Have you been kissed before?'

'No.'

He closed his eyes. Just like he thought. 'Okay. One goodnight kiss.' He knew it was a bad idea, that it would irrevocably change things between them, but damn he wanted to taste her lips, to be her first. He needed it like he needed his next breath.

He shifted and she lifted her head from his chest, allowing him to move over top of her. He hovered over her, lowering himself slowly until their bodies lay flush — his hips aligned with hers, his chest just brushing her hardened nipples and their mouths millimeters from touching. He held himself up on his elbows, and cradled her head in his hands, brushing strands of hair back from her face. Her breath came in fast little puffs against his lips. He took his time, unwilling to rush this. Angling her jaw to his, he lowered down to meet her waiting mouth.

Her lips were full and soft, and he pressed against her, deepening the kiss. Even if part of him knew he shouldn't do this, she deserved to be kissed properly for her first kiss. Cole parted her lips, and when her tongue met his, eager and wet as it swirled against his, his dick went instantly hard again. She didn't kiss like a beginner. He pressed himself into the crook between her legs, and Savannah automatically wrapped her legs around his waist and let out a ragged breath. The heat at her center cradled him and he ground his hips in closer, biting back a moan from the friction. His restraint was dangling by a thread. As fucking amazing as it felt, Cole broke the kiss, knowing he wouldn't be able to stop himself if they kept going. He pressed a chaste kiss to her forehead. 'There, now you've been properly kissed.'

She smiled up at him, her eyes blinking open lazily.

He chuckled at how damn cute she looked, sated and sleepy. 'Just get some rest, okay?'

'Okay.' She rolled to her side, and nuzzled into the pillow.

Chapter 17

That Sunday, like every Sunday, Cole prepared for his visit with Abbie. It wasn't so much that he wanted to go, more like he was obligated. He wouldn't break their weekly appointment simply because he didn't feel like going. Their relationship was much too complex.

He dressed casually, in jeans and a polo shirt. But he added a spray of cologne to his neck just because he knew it made her smile.

'Savannah, I have to go out for a little while. Will you be okay?'

Savannah crossed her arms over her chest and watched as he slipped on a pair of well-worn loafers. 'Of course. I'll be fine.'

'I won't be gone long.'

She glanced around the quiet, empty apartment with a frown. Cole knew it probably wasn't possible for her to feel at home in his stark bachelor pad. She was accustomed to the noise and constant company of living with forty people. The silence stretched between them, and they each refused to break eye contact. He was glad she hadn't asked where he was going. He wouldn't enjoy lying to her. 'I'll only be gone an hour or so.'

Once outside, the sunlight was too bright, casting an overly cheery halo for the occasion. The drive only took ten minutes and Cole parked in front of the building, a familiar knot of uneasiness settling in the pit of his stomach. He always felt dirty when he arrived here, but knew by the time he left, it would be with the relief he craved — however short-lived.

When he returned that afternoon, Cole found Savannah in her bedroom with clothes covering her bed and Cuddles perched on a pillow to supervise. 'What are you doing?'

Savannah glanced up but continued her task. 'Just picking out an outfit for our date. I mean my date with Levi tonight.'

She still wanted to go on the date with Levi? Even after he'd touched her? If he thought it had changed anything between them, he was wrong. It was strange to realize, but he supposed she'd needed the physical release just like he had. Simple as that. 'Is this what you want, Savannah?'

She studied him for a moment, abandoning the stack of jeans and leggings. 'Marissa thought it would be good for me — I've never been on a date before.'

Oh, if Marissa thought it was okay. Damn meddling Marissa. Though he supposed it was good for her to do things any normal nineteen year-old-girl would do. He nodded his okay.

The remainder of the afternoon passed with as little talking as possible. If he could have taken to grunting and pointing, he would have. If Savannah didn't acknowledge what happened between them, he wouldn't either. She must have been more drunk than she'd let on that night. It was a mistake to touch her like he had, to take advantage. It wouldn't happen again, no matter his dick's insistent pleas every time she was near.

Later they met Levi and Deb, his overly sexed mom, in their apartment for a drink before their dinner date. Deb greeted him with a kiss on both cheeks and a squeeze on his ass. He knew he would to be batting her hands off him all night. Not that he really minded a squeeze here or there, he just didn't want to put Savannah in an awkward position. Because he sure as shit wasn't going to be okay with Levi's hands all over Savannah. Just the thought sent Cole's mood south. Levi was her age; Cole should be happy if they hit it off. But the thought of another man touching her made him shudder.

Levi looked Savannah up and down, and Cole cursed his sister yet again for the provocative little outfits she'd picked out. He didn't expect his sister to buy such sexy clothes for Savannah. And fragrant body washes and lotions—his damn bathroom smelled like a girl. He wasn't used to that. Although upon more closely inspecting her, dressed in dark skinny jeans and a turquoise silk blouse that billowed out from her trim figure, he supposed it wasn't all that provocative. It was just Savannah. She was gorgeous. She'd still be gorgeous if she was dressed in a burlap sack.

Savannah fidgeted, tugging on the hem of her top under Levi's inspection. Cole had no doubt that she was unaware of her beauty, the power she held over men. But she'd blossomed like a flower into a beautiful young woman, and he hated that no one had told her that.

Deb was overly made up — wearing a skin tight black dress that barely covered her ass and heels so tall she teetered when she walked. She was trying way too hard. After greetings were exchanged, and Deb had fawned over how pretty Savannah was, they were led into the kitchen.

'What can I get you guys? I have beer, wine…'

'Savannah's not twenty-one,' Cole pointed out.

Deb waved him off. 'Oh relax, we're all going to have a little fun tonight.' Deb handed Savannah a glass of blush-colored wine. 'You always this uptight?' she asked, handing Cole a beer. 'We'll have to work on that.'

'You remember I work for law enforcement, right?'

Deb chuckled, shaking her head and dismissing his comment. Savannah looked down and accepted the wine, but Cole could see the hint of a grin on her face.

He sipped his beer in silence, his eyes following Savannah's movements. She told Deb all about Cuddles and her recent shopping spree with Marissa. Poor Levi had no idea how to get himself into their conversation, and Cole wasn't about to help him. Bastard. He just sat back and enjoyed listening to Savannah. She grew more comfortable, a little more confident with each passing day, her face lighting up as she spoke.

After their drinks, they headed down the parking garage. Cole's Tahoe was large enough for them to ride together. Just before they reached the car, Savannah leaned in close to his ear. 'Are you going to invite Deb over later?'

He turned to study her. 'No. I won't do that again, Savannah. It'll be just you and me tonight.'

Her shoulders visibly relaxed, and she climbed into the backseat with Levi. Cole was thankful that he could keep an eye on things from the rearview mirror, and he noticed Savannah catching his gaze more than once.

They ate at a Mexican restaurant, the four of them squeezed into a booth. He had to hand it to Levi; he'd opened doors and been attentive and kind to Savannah so far. Which was too bad, because Cole was just waiting for the chance to haul off and kick his ass. Though he supposed if he did that, he'd get an earful from Marissa about ruining Savannah's first date. As long as Levi didn't cross the line, he had nothing to worry about.

They dined on tacos, guacamole, and salsa. Deb had ordered a pitcher of margarita's and pushed glass of the icy mixture toward. Savannah. After a few sips she was giggling more than he'd ever seen and knew the tequila was getting to her. Levi used the opportunity to sidle up closer to her. Cole kept one eye on her while he ate, and found that her gaze caught his every few seconds as well.

*

His watchful eyes settled on hers, calming her, providing confidence. She tried to pay attention to Levi, she did, but Cole, trying to delicately eat his grilled shrimp tacos, was too distracting. She'd never really known it was important, but she found herself noticing and appreciating Cole's good table manners. Levi, in comparison, seemed like he was competing for a speed eating title, cramming a large burrito in his mouth and trying to engage her in conversation at the same time. Cole took his time, pausing to participate in a conversation with Deb, dabbing his mouth with a napkin. Savannah wasn't sure why, but seeing Cole outside of his home was fascinating to her.

Deb leaned close to Cole, stealing a tortilla chip from his plate. She leaned in a second time, grazed his neck and told him he smelled good.

Mine. The thought jumped into her mind, unbidden. Savannah tried to focus on her food , but her mind kept wandering to later when she would have Cole all to herself. She wondered if they'd have a repeat of last night. She couldn't stop her gaze from admiring his mouth, remembering how soft it'd felt against hers.

By the end of the meal, Cole was ready to get out of there. Between fighting off Deb and watching after Savannah, he was on edge. He'd never had a table piss him off so bad, but he couldn't see where the fuck Levi's hands were. And the beginning of a headache was piercing his temple.

He paid the bill for the table and stood. 'Ready?'

Deb huffed and slugged back the rest of her margarita. 'Fine.'

Once they got home, he walked through the hall with Deb, ahead of Savannah and Levi, allowing them some semblance of privacy before he took her home. Which he would be doing. He would not stand by and watch Levi try to muscle his way in. Over his dead body.

Once they were finally alone, Cole closed the door while Savannah picked up Cuddles and buried her face in her fur, murmuring baby talk. Cole stood there with a smirk, watching her. Savannah froze, then lowered Cuddles to the ground. His gaze was heavy, and the air crackled between them with the same intensity as last night. He wondered if she was remembering the way he devoured her, flicking his tongue across her swollen pink flesh.

He muttered something about taking Cuddles out for her, and he grabbed the dog to keep from grabbing Savannah. When he came back inside, Savannah had changed into a pair of his sweatpants and a baggy T-shirt and was lying on the couch curled up in a ball, hugging a pillow between her knees.

'What's wrong?'

'My stomach…' she groaned.

'Is it something you ate? Maybe the Mexican food didn't agree with you.'

'No. It's not that. I think it's cramps.'

'Cramps?' Oh. Cramps.

He stared at her for a few minutes, wondering what he could do to ease her discomfort, but for once he was totally out of his league. He pulled his cell from his pocket and dialed Marissa, ducking into the bedroom. 'Hey Rissa.'

'Hey there. You guys go on your double date tonight?'

'Yeah. That worked out fine; but listen, I need your advice. Savannah's lying on the couch and says she has cramps. I thought maybe it was the Mexican food, but she says it's not that.'

Marissa laughed. 'She has cramps — like PMS. She's probably going to start her period, Cole. How long has she been staying with you?'

'About a month.'

'That's what I thought. Okay, here's what you're going to do. First, I put some pads and tampons in her bathroom, so make sure she knows they're there.'

Cole listened, pacing his room as Marissa used words like *heating pad, ibuprofen, warm bath, chick flick* and *ice cream*.

'You got all that?'

'Not really,' he admitted.

'Be nice to her Cole. Being a woman sucks this time of month.'

'Dammit Marissa. No. You talk to her.'

She laughed again. 'Nope. You can handle this.'

'Marissa…' his warning fell on deaf ears as the phone line went dead. 'Dammit all to hell.' He tossed the phone on his bed.

Cole gathered all the supplies and dumped it all on the coffee table in front of her. 'Here. Pain reliever, bottled water, a heating pad, uh…these things.' He pushed the boxes of tampons and pads toward her. 'That should cover it.' He stood and backed away from her as though she was a wild and unpredictable animal.

Her eyes scanned the pile of supplies on the table. 'What's all this?'

'For your…situation,' he mumbled, rubbing the back of this neck.

'Oh, thanks. You didn't have to do that, Cole.'

His posture softened. 'It's fine. And I'm going to run you a warm bath; Marissa said it would help.'

'You called Marissa?'

He nodded.

'Oh.' Her wide eyes followed him from the room.

He filled his large jetted tub with water and a squirt of his body wash to make bubbles. Savannah joined him in the bathroom a few minutes later, watching as he tested the temperature of the water and set out a fresh towel on the counter.

'Thank you.' She planted a damp kiss against his cheek.

He stood stock still as Savannah slipped off the sweatpants and then her panties. Cole turned to give her some privacy as her hands went to the hem of her shirt, but even facing the other direction, her reflection was in full view in the large mirror. She kept her

119

eyes locked on his as she stripped off the shirt, and then her bra, letting all the clothes fall on the floor.

He was secretly glad she had cramps; it meant he wouldn't touch her tonight, as much as he wanted to. But she was undressing in front of him like she had no concept of how little control he had when it came to her.

Savannah stepped carefully into the tub and lowered herself into the water until she was submerged up to her shoulders.

Cole's feet had refused to budge as he watched her undress, but now that she was settled in the water, with her eyes closed and a look of bliss on her face, he felt like he was intruding. He let out a deep sigh of pent up frustration and left Savannah alone to relax.

Cole lay in bed that night with Savannah's warm body cuddled against him and stared up at the ceiling. They couldn't keep living this way. He knew that, yet he didn't want to change a thing. He had Savannah here, safe with him, but he knew he was holding her back. She needed someone to help her experience all life had to offer, to help her grow, not someone who wanted to keep her all to himself. Savannah's breathing hitched and she curled her body tighter around his. He wondered if she still had cramps, and absently rubbed a hand across her lower back, kneading the tight muscles.

Cole made a decision then and there. If he was selfish enough to keep Savannah, he would help her live life, give her all the experiences she never had. He knew that if he really wanted to help her, that meant preparing her to be able to live on her own. And eventually provide for herself, even if he didn't like the idea of her leaving. He wanted her to have the option. Cole closed his eyes and let out a deep breath, relaxing into Savannah's warm embrace and feeling confident that somehow this would all work out.

Cole woke with a start in the darkened room. He glanced at the clock. Two in the morning. He scrubbed a hand across his face and glanced at Savannah. She slept peacefully beside him. It had been over eight months since he'd had one of those nightmares. But the girl that he hadn't been able to save had filtered back into his subconscious, probably provoked by Savannah's rescue. The dreams weren't enough to force him into taking the prescription anti-anxiety pills in his bathroom cabinet, but they were enough to keep him on edge about growing too cozy with Savannah. He needed to stay focused on his job, and that included helping Savannah get on her feet. Nothing more.

Not everything was some damn love story like Marissa thought. Not everyone got their happy endings. He knew that first hand — look at his parents, or go open any of the case files on his desk at work.

He still couldn't help his mind from replaying a thousand scenarios though — each one with him unable to reach Savannah in time and witnessing her dying breath, like he had eight months ago with the other girl. After her death, he'd researched everything he could about the girl who was in the wrong place at the wrong time. Only seventeen, she was downtown because she had a fight with her parents. He closed his eyes and pulled Savannah close, burying his face in her neck, breathing in her scent and trying to escape the vision of the girl from his mind.

Chapter 18

Cole met Marissa at Liam's after work for a quick beer. She'd been bugging him ever since she met Savannah, and he suspected their visit wasn't a friendly sibling get-together. More like a chance get the scoop from him uninterrupted. Liam automatically brought him a beer and Marissa a glass of white wine.

'Thanks man.' He raised his bottle to Liam before bringing it to his lips.

'Sooo,' Marissa drew out the word, smiling at him. 'What's new?'

'Nothing.'

'How's Savannah?'

'Good.'

She pouted. He knew his one-word answers weren't going to fly, but he didn't care. He didn't even understand what was going on between him and Savannah, let alone trying to explain it to someone else.

'How was your date with Sali?'

'Fine.' The only thing he remembered about his date with Sali was what happened afterwards with Savannah. Her dark smoldering eyes watching him fuck another woman was probably the most erotic experience of his life. A flush of heat crawled up his neck at the memory.

'Do you think you'll see her again?'

Sali? 'Nope.'

Marissa rolled her eyes. 'Cole. Talk to me. What's going on with you and Savannah? Are you just planning to support her, or is she going to get a job? Don't take this the wrong way because I really like Savannah, but you're my brother. It's my job to look out for you.'

Cole nearly laughed at the absurdity of her question. 'Savannah's not like that. She's not after my money — not that I have much of it anyway—and yes I do plan to support her for as long as she needs it.' He took another sip of his beer, growing agitated at where the conversation was headed. He expected Marissa to probe into his love life like she usually did, not warn him away from Savannah.

'That's a lot to ask of you, Cole.'

'She's not a burden, Rissa.' *Quite the opposite, in fact.* 'I like having her there.'

A knowing smile stretched across her lips. 'What's really going on between you two?'

'She was completely broken when I found her. I won't take advantage of her. Let it go.'

Marissa laughed. 'You're as blind as a damn bat. I've seen the way she looks at you, Cole. I don't think you can take advantage of the willing.'

What did that mean? How did Savannah look at him? 'She doesn't look at me any such way.' *Did she?*

Marissa chuckled again, then took another sip of her wine. 'She looks at you like she wants a taste. And don't get me started on how she cooks and cleans for you and basically waits on you hand and foot.'

'You're reading too much into this.' Savannah did those things because they gave her something to do, allowed her to feel useful. That had nothing to do with him, did it?

'You called me in a panic when she had cramps. You don't find that …odd?'

He shrugged, refusing to answer and focused on his beer. He hadn't thought it was odd at the time, but he could see how it probably seemed like something a concerned boyfriend would do.

'Dammit Cole, she's not the one who's broken—you are. I swear you could be in love with her and not even know it with that thick head of yours.'

Not likely. Cole intended to laugh and brush her comment off, but his mouth had gone bone dry. He pulled down another sip of his beer, praying the icy liquid would clear his brain of all the impossible thoughts.

'What would you think about me getting my driver's license?' Savannah asked over breakfast the following morning.

Hot coffee slid painfully down the wrong pipe. Cole struggled to clear his airway, unable to speak for nearly a minute.

Savannah set the spatula beside the skillet of eggs, anchored a hand on her hip, and launched into a speech. 'I've driven before. Plenty of times. I learned on the old pickup truck we had on the compound.'

Setting his mug down and clearing his throat, Cole nodded. 'That's fine, Savannah. I'll set up the appointment for a driver's ed course.'

With Marissa's words from the night before urging him on, and the topic of her future already broached, Cole considered how to bring up the idea of Savannah getting a job. He didn't know what the right thing was, hell, he could pay her for cooking and cleaning his house, but he knew that wasn't why she did those things and didn't want to insult her. He knew she was good with animals, baking and cooking. Certainly there were things she could do, and perhaps even go to school if she was interested. 'Once you get your license, you'll be able to get out when I'm at work.' He poked at the second slice of banana bread Savannah had set in front of him. 'Have you thought about what you might want to do?' He dared a glance up at her.

'I'd like to work with children. Perhaps babysitting, or maybe at a daycare center.'

'That's a great idea.' Cole was surprised how easily the conversation had gone. Maybe Savannah was ready for more, stronger than he had given her credit for. He headed into his bedroom to continue getting ready for work, feeling somehow uneasy about the conversation they just had.

As much as Savannah wanted to admit she was just as unaffected by Cole as he seemed by her, she couldn't. Especially since watching him with that other woman had shattered her heart into a million tiny pieces. She had stupidly started to fall for him, his gentle affections, his caring nature, his strong work ethic, all of him And ever since she watched him make love to the other girl, her body had joined forces with her heart, the ache now all-encompassing, possessing her from the inside out.

She missed him when he was at work. Missed his scent, his warmth and just having someone else to share little things with. Like when Cuddles jumped up on the couch for the first time— confused at how she'd gotten up there—or when she finally mastered the recipe for her favorite pie that her friend Melody used to make for her.

She practically mauled him when he got home from work, desperate for contact and attention. And he always allowed it, but never encouraged anything further between them. Savannah knew it was time for her to find a job — to have something to devote her time and attention to that would be worthwhile, rather than mothering Cole to death. Though he never complained.

But even as she planned the future, she couldn't keep her thoughts from wandering to Cole. The way his dark intense eyes felt on her skin, his casual brushes of contact…she doubted he had any idea how insane they made her. The way he smiled when he took the first bite of a meal she'd cooked, the way he looked with his shirt sleeves rolled up when he got home from work. She found just about everything he did sexy. And don't get her started on his scent when he arrived home from the gym, skin glistening, and gym shorts hanging loose on his hips. It took every ounce of strength she possessed not to jump him.

She'd never had feelings like this before—not about anyone—and had finally mustered up to the courage to talk to her therapist about it last week. He'd assured her that her feelings for the opposite sex were entirely normal and to be expected, living in close quarters with someone she was attracted to. But he'd cautioned her about getting involved with Cole, saying that if he didn't return her feelings, Savannah would get hurt.

Savannah had laid herself bare for Cole and little good it had done. Sure he had been tempted enough to kiss her in all the right spots until she dissolved into pleasure, but then he'd pulled her panties into place and left like nothing had happened between them. It seemed like nothing she did made him see her like a woman. He still saw that scared, life-weary girl he'd rescued. When he'd finally kissed her—a full, sensuous open-mouthed kiss—she could tell it affected him, yet he wouldn't let himself go there with her. She'd briefly wondered if perhaps he was gay, but she knew he took simple pleasures from their contact, even if that was all it was — the warmth of another body. So she'd gone on the date with Levi, and then this morning she'd talked to Cole about getting a driver's license and her own job. It was time to think about her future, as scary as that might be. And not just because it meant relying only on herself, but because the thought of being away from Cole felt like a loss she couldn't handle. She'd been falling for him since that first moment she'd seen him—weapon drawn, and his dark, intelligent eyes swept the room where she hid.

When Cole left for work that morning, she cleaned the kitchen, polished the black granite countertops, and then positioned herself at the dining room table with his laptop. She began looking for jobs and researching the cost of apartments. It was time to make a plan for herself. She couldn't rely on Cole's generosity forever.

Chapter 19

Cole thought yoga was supposed to relax you, which was why he couldn't understand why Savannah had come home madder than a hornet's nest.

She tossed her yoga mat in the front closet, and then retreated to the kitchen. Cole had figured she would have joined him in the living room to tell him all about it, talking in her excited way whenever she had a new experience. He glanced at his watch. Dinnertime…maybe she was anxious to begin cooking. But it didn't sound like she was cooking so much as punishing the dishes.

'Savannah?' Cole rounded the corner to the kitchen, where the sound of clattering pots and pans was starting to alarm him.

'What?' she turned briskly, holding a large chef's knife in her hand.

'Whoa.' He held up his hands. 'I just wanted to see how yoga went.'

She narrowed her eyes, refusing to lower the knife. 'Fine,' she bit out in a clipped tone.

He took a step back. 'Did, ah, something happen?' His brows knitted together in concern.

'Nope.' She slashed through a ripe tomato with such force, a spray of seeds and juice misted the countertop.

'You sure?' He dared a step closer. 'Did you have…fun?'

She was still dressed for a work out, a pair of skin tight black pants hugging her ass in the most distracting way. God bless whoever invented yoga pants. Her little white tank was riding up, exposing a strip of her narrow waist and lower back. Visions of caressing that ass in his palms, along with memories of the way her skin tasted, danced through his subconscious.

Dear God he wanted her.

Bad.

He'd been trying to avoid being alone with her ever since he'd surrendered and brought her pleasure. As much as he wanted a repeat, he hadn't dared give in. All this past week, he worked late, hit the gym after work, went to Liam's pub for a drink, then came home and slipped into bed while she was sleeping. Of course, that hadn't stopped her from curling her body around his, releasing a happy little sigh against his chest, or pulling his arm around her so they could spoon. She certainly wasn't shy about taking what she needed in terms of physical affection, but neither had actually communicated about their *relationship*, or whatever this thing was between them.

She dropped the knife, letting it clatter against the cutting board, her task momentarily forgotten. 'Fun? Hmm, let's see. Was it fun to see the girl you brought home twisting her body into impossible poses for ninety minutes? No. I don't suppose it was.'

'Savannah.' His tone was sharp and she met his eyes.

'What Cole? What?'

He swallowed and tested the ground between them by taking another step closer. 'First, give me the knife.' His grip closed around her wrist and with his free hand, he slid the knife further away from her, just in case. He'd never seen her so worked up. They were standing just inches apart and Cole could feel the heat of her skin radiating off her. He could smell the sweet floral notes of her shampoo assaulting his resolve. He imagined leaning in and possessing her mouth in a kiss. He wanted to feel her full lips part for him, accept him, and remembering the way her little soft tongue rubbed against his made his balls ache. But even as he processed all this, in just two-heartbeat's time, he knew he wouldn't kiss her. Instead he squeezed his eyes closed, willing his hard-on to relent. 'Tell me what's really bothering you.'

Savannah looked down, at war with herself over what to say next. What could she say to the man who made her feel so cared for one minute and so furious the next. She didn't want to seem ungrateful, but something had to give between them. She needed to understand what was running through his head. She'd struggled through that night's yoga lesson, hating that she had to watch the instructor he'd slept with move her lithe body in all sorts of positions. Why did he bring her home, bring her here to live with him in the first place? Why go through all this trouble if he didn't really want her? 'If you don't want me— why didn't you just leave me where I was?' She looked down, unable to meet his eyes, yet desperately seeking a reaction.

'Left you there? Are you crazy? That asshole Jacob was a whackjob. You should be thanking me for getting you out of there.'

'Thanking you for tearing apart the only family I knew? For bringing me here where I can do nothing but sit and worry and reflect on everything I lost?' A silent tear skittered down her cheek before the back of her hand caught it.

'I *had* to get you out of there, and I don't regret bringing you here either.' He sighed. 'I know there must be things…people you miss.'

She swallowed a lump in her throat, a new rush of emotion washing over her. 'I was this close to having Calista potty trained.' She held her fingers an inch apart. She missed that feisty two-year-old with a mass of untamed blond curls. 'She called me Vannah since she couldn't say my name. And Melody, the oldest member, was my only source of sanity. She was the only one who could get Jacob to see reason. Her blackberry pie was my favorite. I had this theory that her pie alone could solve most of the world's problems.'

Cole smiled and took her hand. 'I remember reading about Melody in the case file. She's living with her adult daughter in Denver now.'

Savannah's heart jumped in her chest. Melody and her daughter had a falling out years ago. She was happy to hear they were reunited. She knew everyone was going on with their lives, and she needed to as well. But it was just so hard. She hated not knowing what would come next for her and Cole.

She stared defiantly at him, urging him to say something, anything that might explain what was happening between them, but he remained silent, his expression weary and unsure.

At a loss for what to say to comfort Savannah, Cole dropped his gaze and rubbed a hand along the back of his neck. 'Go shower. I'll order out for dinner tonight.' He released her and Savannah stumbled away on seemingly shaky legs —from the yoga workout or from the desire escalating between them, he wasn't sure.

He took a deep breath, trying to calm his frazzled nerves. If things got any more heated, he'd erupt in flames. He dug out his cell phone and called in an order for Chinese food.

When Cole got in bed that night, Cuddles was sprawled out in the middle. He couldn't help but wonder if Savannah had placed the dog in bed to create a physical between them. He lifted the sheet and pulled the comforter toward him, being none to gentle about disturbing the dog. Part of him hoped the damn thing would saunter back into its kennel in the guest room where it usually slept. The beast was a little cock-block.

Chapter 20

The next few weeks passed by in the same sort of careful avoidance. They continued to sleep together in Cole's bed each night, but other than the cuddling, nothing physical had happened. Cole was sure Savannah had no idea how badly he wanted her; especially when she walked that fine little panty-clad ass around in front of him, or emerged from his bathroom only wearing a towel, still damp and pink from the shower. It took every ounce of self-control he possessed not to pick her up, strip her of the towel, and pound into her again and again until he came.

The littlest things were starting to set him off and he was pleasuring himself more than he had since he was a teenager Yet it brought little relief to the pent up desire he harbored for her. But he wouldn't fuck her. She deserved so much more than he was prepared to offer.

Even with the daily temptations, the weeks had passed by quickly. Savannah had graduated from her driving course, and last Saturday he'd taken her to get her license.

After picking out a car for Savannah — a year old silver sedan that he was able to negotiate down in price—Cole signed the paperwork and wrote out a check for the down-payment. The car was nothing fancy, but you wouldn't know that by looking at Savannah. After finishing up inside, he found her still sitting in the driver's seat, inspecting every inch of the car — flipping on the headlights, opening and closing the various compartments as if it was the most magnificent thing she'd ever seen.

She peered at Cole as he approached the open driver's side door. 'Do you like it?' he asked, even though it was obvious she did.

'I don't just like it. This is love.' She ran her hand gently across the dash.

'Good. Because you've got to drive it home.'

Her eyes filled with gratitude and she nodded. 'Can we stop on the way home and go out to lunch? Sort of a mini celebration?'

Cole glanced at his watch. 'Actually…I have somewhere I need to go.'

She frowned and fiddled with the keys. 'Oh, right…it's Sunday.'

He nodded wordlessly, his mouth going dry. He'd been waiting for her to ask about where he went every Sunday, but so far she hadn't. And there was no way he was offering that information up voluntarily. Savannah didn't say anything else; she just pulled the door closed of her little silver sedan and started the engine.

Cole climbed into his SUV and adjusted his rear-view mirror so he could look back at Savannah. She looked so small sitting in the car, her head poking above the steering wheel. A pang of nervous panic hit him like a wave. He would figure all this out. He had to. But first he needed to go see his ex. He gripped the steering wheel and left the parking lot.

Chapter 21

Savannah slipped out of bed, leaving Cole to sleep a little longer. He looked so at ease when he slept, so carefree, she couldn't bring herself to wake him even though he was already running late for work.

She made coffee and scrambled eggs, adding a palmful of shredded cheese they way he liked it. Just as the toast popped from the toaster, Cole emerged from the bedroom, his hair rumpled like a little boy's. It did funny things to Savannah's stomach. She wanted to rake her hands through that hair, and plant a kiss on his mouth. Instead she stood there watching him.

'Why didn't you wake me?' he asked, running a hand across his hair, though his attempt at smoothing it was pointless. Eight hours of sleep had styled it for him. None of his attempts would change that.

'I was about to. Breakfast is ready.'

He settled in at a bar stool while Savannah poured him a cup of coffee and placed the steaming mug in front of him.

'Thanks,' he mumbled.

She knew from experience he'd be worthless until he had drank at least half a cup. She took her time plating his breakfast, allowing him to enjoy his coffee in silence. He placed he napkin across his lap and met Savannah's eyes as she set the plate down in front of him.

'You're welcome.' She busied her hands, adding some eggs to her own plate before joining him at the island. She could smell his manly scent — a mix of his spicy aftershave, a hint of soap and something else that was uniquely Cole. She hated the way it made her belly flutter and her fingers stumble over her task. But she managed to lower her plate to the counter successfully and settled on the stool next to him.

They ate in silence and Savannah was grateful. Cole was introspective and quiet, and it was times like this she found herself wondering what else she didn't know about this man. Her mind drifted to Cole's disappearances on Sunday afternoons. She was curious, but she hadn't come right out and asked him. She was grateful for Cole and everything he'd done for her. Somehow she knew he would tell her eventually, when he was ready. Until then, she would force that from her mind and move forward with her life. She wouldn't bombard Cole with questions, not when he'd been so gentle and careful with her past. And she wouldn't let her past sabotage her chance at a happy future.

After breakfast, Savannah wordlessly scooped Cuddles up into her arms and rocked the puppy silently against her chest. Unwilling in that moment to go to Cole for comfort, like she instinctually wanted to, she instead settled for the sweet puppy's affections. She wanted Cole to wrap her in his arms and kiss away her pain. But he remained seated at the island, stabbing at his breakfast like he was thinking just as hard as she was.

As badly as Savannah wanted to believe she was healed, whole again, she knew it wasn't true. She still had occasional nightmares about living at the compound, about Dillon coming after her like he'd promised. And she still dreamed about her mom's deadly aneurysm, waking teary and shaking. She'd push those thoughts away, burying the ache, and nestle closer into Cole's arms those nights. That was the past, and she wouldn't let it hurt her. In her waking hours, her fear was different. So acute she could reach out and touch it. She was afraid of being alone. She wanted Cole to notice her like a man should, take her in his arms, make her feel desired, whole again. But each time she tried to show him what she needed, tempt him by curling her body around his, as if to provide him a hint of what she craved, he'd stiffen as though he was in pain and bark out an excuse to remove her hands. His rejection was slowly ruining her, causing her to wonder why she didn't fit in anywhere — why she wasn't wanted.

Perhaps if she could break down his barrier, she could show Cole how good they could be together. It might not change anything, but maybe it would. Maybe he would finally see how much she cared for him and admit he had feelings for her too.

Chapter 22

This was a stupid idea.

Cole peeked over at Savannah, wondering if she could sense his anxious mood, but she didn't seem to suspect a thing. She watched the traffic out the passenger window and hummed along to the radio.

He'd gotten her out of the house on the pretext of taking her out for a birthday lunch. It wasn't a complete lie. Lunch would be involved, but that wasn't the focus.

When he parked in front of the roller rink, he glanced at Savannah

She sat up straighter and stared at the building, eyebrows raised in surprise. 'Cole?'

Cole hopped out of the truck and opened her door. 'Just come on.'

She accepted his hand, letting him pull her from the car. 'But what are we doing here?'

'You'll see.' He pressed his mouth into a line as the overwhelming desire to grin like an idiot struck him. He paid for their admission and led a very wide-eyed and confused Savannah through the skating rink.

The lights inside the rink were dimmed, and flashes of blues and greens sparkled across the polished wood floor, bathing the skaters in color as they whirled by. Pop music drowned out all conversation and kept Savannah quiet as she took in their surroundings. She'd stopped walking to watch a line of skaters fly past her on the way to the rink. Cole grabbed her hand to urge her on. He led Savannah to the back party-room he'd rented. Marissa had coordinated most of the details, but it was his idea to throw her a party. When Marissa mentioned the skating party she had when she was ten, Cole latched on to the idea. He liked that he could give her a childhood experience she'd missed out on, and maybe even teach her to skate. He also thought it was the perfect venue to reunite Savannah with the children she still thought about daily. He didn't know if Savannah would break down at seeing everyone, but hoped they'd at least be happy tears. He wanted her to enjoy her birthday, not have a sob-fest on his hands. But her hesitation and sudden silence had him wondering if he'd made the right call.

With one hand still holding Savannah's, he opened the door to the private room. They were greeted by an explosion of pink. Balloons, crepe paper streamers, a happy birthday sign strung from the ceiling, and a platter of pink frosted cupcakes sat on the table.

'Surprise!' A dozen or so voices squealed in unison.

Savannah's mouth gaped, no sound escaping as she took in the little faces in front of her. Then she dropped to her knees and released an exhale, like she'd been holding her breath for weeks.

The children ran to her, overwhelming her and knocking her back as they climbed into her waiting arms. Savannah's smile was as big as he'd ever seen it and silent tears leaked from the corners of her eyes.

He knew it was slightly risky tracking down the families with children, sending them an invite to Savannah's birthday party, but the risk had been worth it — especially seeing Savannah so happy. He'd promised to pay their admission and skate rentals, and almost everyone had agreed to come. Watching their reunion made the cost well worth it.

Once Savannah was freed from the pile on the floor, she launched herself into Cole's arms, holding him tight, so tight he couldn't breathe. No words could adequately express how much seeing the children meant to her.

He l gently kissed her temple. 'Happy Birthday, Savannah.'

Her mouth curved into a smile and all his fears about this being a dumb idea dissolved away.

They spent the afternoon skating —well, wobbling across the slickened floor in rollerblades, which none of the children or their mothers had used before, and eating pizza and cupcakes. Cole attempted to teach Savannah to skate; a task made more difficult with children wrapped around their legs.

By the end of the day, a rosy-cheeked Savannah said her good-byes, and exchanged email addresses with several of the women before following Cole to his car. It seemed that today had given her some of the closure she needed — the ability to see with her own eyes that everyone was alive and well. The deep satisfaction glowing on her features was all the thank you Cole needed.

Chapter 23

Savannah returned home from her first day of work to find Cole home earlier than usual. and stationed in the kitchen, over a pot of spaghetti.

'Hey there,' he grinned, wiping his hands on a dishtowel before coming to greet her. 'How was it?' He tipped her chin up, scrutinizing her expression.

She threw her arms around his midsection, burying her face against his chest. 'It was amazing. I was so nervous at first, even to make small talk with the girls that work there, but being with the babies all day, changing diapers, rocking them, giving them bottles, playing…it was so fun!'

Cole rocked back on his heels and smiled at her. 'Good.' He tucked a lock of hair behind her ear. 'I'm proud of you, Savannah.'

His words did more to sooth her soul than he could have known. No one had ever told her that before. She remained immobile, looking into his dark eyes, soaking up the attention. After several seconds though, Cole hadn't looked away, and she grew anxious under his intense stare. She licked her lips and took a step back, her eyes darting for the kitchen, needing to be anywhere but on his. 'Did you, um, cook?' she asked, thoroughly confused.

He laughed, easy and carefree. 'Yeah, I tried. It's your first day of work, so I, uh wanted to surprise you.'

'Oh.'

He led the way to the kitchen and Savannah dutifully followed. 'It's just pasta and tomato sauce, don't get too excited.'

'It smells great. I think we have garlic bread in the freezer. And I could whip up a salad.' She started for the fridge.

His hands on her waist stopped her. 'Nope. This is my plan. Out.' He gave her a playful shove toward the dining room. 'I got this.'

Savannah laughed but obeyed. 'Okay.' She held up her hands. 'I'll just go change, if that's okay. I have spit-up from at least three different babies on my shirt.'

Cole chuckled as she made her way into the guest bedroom. Once inside, she stripped herself of the jeans and long-sleeved T-shirt she'd worn to work, and after a perusal of her closet, she decided on a quick shower. The pasta was still boiling, so she had a few minutes at least.

She twisted her hair into a messy knot and felt the temperature of the water. It was warm and inviting. Savannah stepped into the glass-enclosed shower, grabbed her loofa, and poured a glob of her jasmine-scented body wash onto it. She scrubbed her entire body twice, enjoying the water. She smiled at the memory of being the only one able to soothe the fussy, teething Bella at work today. She'd always had a special gift with infants. They were as comfortable with her as she was with them. Savannah washed her face, scrubbing away the day, before turning around to feel the water beat between her shoulder blades. Hmm. That felt nice. It turned out, rocking and holding babies all day was hard work. But satisfying.

Savannah turned off the water, dried herself with one of the oversized bath sheets Cole used for towels and then dressed in her favorite pajamas — a pair of shorts and one of Cole's worn T-shirts.

She returned to the kitchen after freeing her hair and combing out the snarls. 'Mmm. Smells great in here.'

Cole was just plating the pasta and thick slices of garlic bread when she approached the dining room table. He hadn't taken her suggestion of a salad, but that was okay, this was plenty as it was. 'Sit down.' He gestured, pulling out her seat.

Savannah obeyed, easing down into the seat. 'Thank you for cooking,' she murmured, surveying the food in front of her. It looked delicious and smelled even better.

'Wait. One more thing.' Cole returned carrying a bottle of red wine in the crook of his elbow and two wine glasses. Savannah eyed him curiously, but he just shrugged. 'What? It's a special occasion.'

Her mouth twitched with a smile as he poured them each a glass of the ruby-colored wine. 'For you.' He placed the glass in front of her.

'Thank you.' It all felt sophisticated and elegant, having Cole wait on her, and she giggled at the pleasure in this moment.

His eyes flashed to hers. 'What?'

'Nothing,' she replied, fixing on a straight face.

Cole tempted her to respond, his dark eyes locked on hers for a moment too long, before he finally pulled out his own chair and sat beside her. 'So you liked the daycare?' he asked around a bite of garlic bread.

'I loved it. It's so fun watching them learn and play at this age. And then when they get older, watching them grow and discover new things. I think this is the perfect job for me. It's basically what I did at the compound, but I never got paid for it.'

He nodded, taking a sip of his wine. 'Then I'm happy for you.'

Why did he sound so cold? And why didn't his smile reach his eyes? He'd been the one to encourage her to get a job, and now that she had one she liked, he was acting all strange about it. She stuffed a big bite of pasta into her mouth, realizing she was famished and not all that concerned with acting lady-like around him. A healthy sip of red wine followed. Hmm. Sweeter than she expected. So he'd cooked, and opened a bottle of wine? Big deal. It didn't make him acting all weird okay.

She ignored his strange mood and relayed the specifics of her day, the regimented schedule at the daycare: nine a.m. breakfast, then a diaper change, followed by morning nap, then playtime till lunch, and then the schedule repeated itself- eat, diapers, nap, play, before the parent pickup. She laughed just thinking about it. It had been a full and busy day. But fun.

'Do you want kids?' she asked, placing her fork beside her cleared plate.

His eyes flashed with alarm. 'Never really thought about it, why?'

She frowned and bit her lip. 'You're twenty-seven; how have you never thought about it?'

'You sound just like Marissa,' he muttered under his breath as he carried the plates to the sink.

Savannah remained seated at the table, her face burning like someone had slapped her. What was with him tonight? She finished her wine, trying to regain her composure before joining him in the kitchen. He glanced at her empty glass and refilled it. 'Go relax.' He was acting sweet, but his words…his words felt cold and abrasive.

'It's okay. I'd rather help,' she replied, her voice coming out soft and unsure.

They stood side by side at the sink, Savannah passing Cole each dish to load the dishwasher. She was hyper-aware of him: his toned forearms, his masculine scent and muscular physique that towered over hers.

After finishing the dishes in silence, they retired to the couch and Cole turned on a movie. It was all she was in the mood for— lounging on the couch—since the combination of working all day and the wine had her feeling drained, but in a good way. Cole settled next to her, keeping his distance, but continually refilling their glasses with wine. By the end of the movie she was buzzed. And dear God help her, she was horny.

She set her empty glass on the table, and laid her head in Cole's lap. His hands found their way under her hair, massaging her neck. 'You're tense,' he whispered.

She sat up suddenly, face-to-face with him. 'You're acting weird tonight.' She cringed. She hadn't meant to blurt it out that way.

'I'm sorry. You didn't deserve that.'

She wanted to ask him why, what was wrong, but he brought his hand up to cup her cheek, and her eyes fluttered closed at the touch. His thumb gently stroked her face, the roughened callus skimming along her skin in the most tender way imaginable. And all was forgiven.

'For the record, I am happy for you,' he breathed, his mouth just inches from hers.

Savannah shifted; a desperate need to get closer urged her into his lap. Straddling him, she placed her hands on the back of the couch, gripping the leather to avoid running her hands through his hair. Savannah licked her bottom lip, silently begging him to kiss her. Cole's eyes caught the movement and his gaze centered on her mouth. Exactly where she wanted him. His hands came up around her ribcage, not pulling her closer, not pushing her away, just holding her in place against him. His thumb skittered across her side, gently stroking her over her T-shirt, so close to her breast, yet still way too far away.

Their eyes met and Savannah thought she might dissolve into a puddle if he kept looking at her like that. His eyes were dark with desire, which only fueled her desperate need for him. If he didn't kiss her soon, she would combust. Of that she was certain. 'Cole…' His name on her lips was a silent plea, a begging desperation that could only be answered one way.

Cole gripped the back of her neck with one hand, his other still planted on her waist and pulled her mouth to his. His kiss was nothing like the last time, his mouth met hers in a desperate rush, wasting no time parting her lips, gliding his tongue along hers, and tilting her jaw to take what he needed. He was needy and merciless, nipping at her bottom lip and grinding his hips into hers. Her eyes drifted closed in pure bliss and she turned her mind off to every thought but one. *Cole.*

His hands on her shoulders reluctantly pushed her away, her lips still damp and tingling from the passion behind his kisses. She fought to catch her breath, to understand why he'd stopped.

'I'm sorry, Savannah. I can't,' he whispered, his voice thick with tension.

His words weren't necessary, the faraway look in his eyes confirmed the moment had passed. He was pulling away from her. Once again. With a heavy heart, she disentangled herself from his lap and headed for the guest room. She curled into a ball in the center of the bed, pulling Cuddles up against her body and released a heavy sigh. She struggled to understand their complicated relationship, dividing her feelings into different compartments so she could examine each one, just like Dr. White had taught her. First there was admiration, then attraction, then disappointment. What that all added up to, she had no idea. But each time Cole showed a glimpse of interest, only to pull away, was eventually going to ruin her. That much was certain.

Chapter 24

Tonight was a bad idea. Of course Cole realized that much too late. Liam, Marissa, Marissa's good friend Kelly, and Savannah all sat around the table enjoying drinks and friendly banter. Well, everyone *else* was enjoying those things. Savannah's posture was stiff, her arms crossed over her chest, and her expression was pinched.

The plan was to celebrate Savannah's new job. Cole's plan did not include Kelly shooting Savannah bitchy looks and rubbing his thigh under the table. *Damn, couldn't a man enjoy a beer in peace?* He was already looking forward to later, just him and Savannah in the quiet solitude of home.

Savannah's gaze lingered suspiciously on Kelly, Marissa's very pretty blond friend, who was flirting with him ruthlessly—slowly eating the olives from her martini while her eyes remained locked on Cole's, seductively swaying her hips when she crossed the room, leaning in close, whispering while curling her hand around his bicep.

After several minutes, Savannah excused herself, fleeing from the table as if her life depended on it.

'Excuse me.' Cole jogged after her. He caught up to Savannah at the bar, where she stood with her back to him. She stiffened when his body heat invaded her space, sensing he was near.

'Have you slept with her?' she asked, her voice small.

Shit. 'Kelly?'

She turned to face him and nodded.

'Yes. A long time ago.'

'More than once?'

Cole nodded. A couple of times. Drunkenly.

Savannah turned, storming away from him. *What in the world?*

Cole caught up to her near the restrooms and gripped her elbow. If she thought she could escape him, she was wrong. He knew every nook and cranny of Liam's bar, and he wasn't opposed to going into the ladies room after her if that's what it took. 'Savannah, wait. Why are you upset?'

She drew in a shaky breath, her chest heaving with the effort.

He'd never seen her angry before, but she seemed to be having trouble keeping herself in check. 'Tell me,' he commanded.

Tears swam in her eyes, but she didn't run, didn't try to escape again. 'Can I please be around just one woman you haven't touched? Is that too much to ask?' Her voice was full of anger, her eyes blazing on his.

'There's Marissa.' He nodded toward his sister, who watched them wearily, like she'd been waiting for this to blow up in his face.

Savannah sighed, exasperated. 'Right, Marissa — the only person you'll share yourself with *emotionally*.'

Cole's brow crinkled in confusion. 'Savannah.' Her name on his lips was a broken plea. He knew it wouldn't take much convincing before he gave into the physical, but a real emotional commitment? No. He couldn't. 'I'm sorry I can't change the past and who I've slept with. I'm sorry, okay?'

'What are we doing, Cole?' Her question pushed against his carefully constructed wall. And when he met her eyes, like a crack of thunder through a vacant sky, he understood. Saw her and all her antics with new eyes. Did Savannah want him? She couldn't. Not like that. What did she even know about being with a man?

Especially a man like him? Work came first, relationships second, love maybe not at all.

Cole looked back at their table. Liam, Marissa and Kelly were all gawking at them. *Shit*. 'Come here.' He took Savannah's hand and pulled her further down the back hallway that led to the restrooms. It wasn't private, but at least they wouldn't have a table of spectators. Once it was just the two of them in the dimly lit hallway, Cole could feel the heat from her skin, smell the scent of her shampoo, and see the pulse thrumming in her neck. Maybe privacy was a bad idea.

They were barely out of sight, and Savannah was in his arms. She didn't want to need him like this—to use him for her comfort—but she had little choice.

'Savannah…' He dislodged her hands from around his waist, holding her at arm's length. 'Tell me what you're thinking.'

She hated the way her body betrayed her when Cole was near. Especially since he was so oblivious to her. She released her hold on him, clasping her hands in front of her. 'I'm sorry, this is hard for me. I just hate knowing that you touched her.' She looked down, unable to meet his eyes, too nervous to see his reaction. She'd struggled all night to figure out what his motivation was. Why did he bring her home in the first place? Why plan this celebration for her?

'I'm sorry.' He sighed. 'That happened before I ever knew you. It was a long time ago, and it won't happen again.'

She swallowed a lump in her throat, trying to talk herself out of feeling so emotional, but it was no use. She wanted more from Cole. She needed more. And she had no idea how to tell him. She would have to show him. She couldn't keep living like this.

He opened his arms, seeming to sense the shift in her mood. 'Come here.'

Her heart rate kicked up and she stepped into his arms, allowing him to hold her. And all was right with the world. She closed her eyes and rested her head on his chest.

Why did he keep fucking up with her? He needed to get his body in check, not allow it to react when she was near. She was soft and innocent and needing comforting — that was all. What she did not need was him getting wood every time she was in the room. Christ, what was he, seventeen? His hands smoothed over her bare arms. She was so soft, so lovely and she felt so familiar to him, molded to his body like this.

'Just take me home…' she murmured lightly, still resting her head against his chest.

He wouldn't push her to stay out. Tonight was supposed to be about her — a celebration to show her he was proud, but he could tell it was too much too fast. She wasn't ready. 'Tell me what's wrong first.' He struggled to keep his pulse under control and waited for her response. He knew that whatever Savannah wanted he would give her. And that fucking terrified him.

'I want all of this, I do. My own life, a job, an apartment. I want to live, Cole. Fully live. Not have you watching me every second for signs that I'm about to lose it. Who knows, maybe I will at some point; but we all do sometimes, right?' He didn't know if that was a jab at him, and his own nightmares. He raised his hand as if to stop her, but Savannah pushed it away, and continued. 'And I need you, Cole.'

'You have me,' he murmured, bringing a hand to her waist. 'You know that, right? Christ Savannah, give me a break. This is uncharted territory for me, but you have to know that I'd do anything for you. I'll do anything to keep you safe and protected.'

'Cole…' her voice was a soft plea. 'I need more than that. You must know how I feel about you…'

Her confession floored him. How had they gotten here? Then he remembered the meals she'd lovingly prepared for him, the puppy he'd brought home for her, the new wardrobe, running her bubble baths. *Shit.* He never intended for her to read more into it. She deserved taking care of, especially in the fragile state she'd been in.

He closed his eyes, preparing to explain to her why that could never happen, yet failing to find the words, failing to find a single reason why he shouldn't take her home right now and strip her naked. She couldn't possibly understand the crazy things that swirled through his head, how hard she was to resist for all these many weeks.

She stepped in closer, testing his resolve. 'Please Cole.'

He could no longer deny the compelling feeling that she was supposed to be his. He felt the first pang of it when he found her in that dingy back bedroom. She was the brightest thing in that place — a light of wonder emanating from her green eyes even that day as she drank him in. And as hard as he'd fought it, every day he spent with Savannah only secured her place in his heart a little more. 'If we do this… it's on my terms, Savannah.'

She nodded, even though her eyes betrayed her confusion. But it was enough of an agreement for him. He could end it at any time. He would call the shots. 'Come on.' He grabbed her hand, lacing their fingers and roughly pulled her toward the exit.

'What about…' She gestured to the table.

'I'll text Marissa and tell her you weren't feeling well.'

She nodded and allowed him to guide her to the door.

Once they were inside Cole's bedroom, the air between them hung thick with anticipation. Though they had shared his bed for several weeks now, this felt like something else entirely. Something pre-mediated. Cole took an uneasy step toward her. The thought of taking their easy relationship somewhere new scared him, and he couldn't say why. But when Savannah bit into her soft bottom lip and her gaze fell to his belt buckle, all coherent thoughts escaped him. He'd wanted this for too long, and now she was offering herself up to him.

He waited to see what she would do. It was the one promise he'd make himself. It would have to be her. She'd have to make the first move if she really wanted him. But then he supposed she already had. Wasn't that what the night with Sali had been about? She watched from the doorway and when he went to her room… she'd been the one to remove her shirt, to tell him, wordlessly what she wanted. He'd listened, on some primitive level, and obeyed enough to give her what that moment required, but nothing more. He didn't take her then. And wouldn't now unless he knew it was exactly what she wanted.

When Savannah ventured a step closer to him and her eyes raked over his body, all self-control was lost. 'I'm done, Savannah. I'm done resisting you. I'm done pretending I don't want this.'

She whimpered softly and met his eyes. Hers were wide with fear…or curiosity, he didn't know which. Didn't care. He needed to be inside her.

'Take off your top,' he ordered.

Savannah lifted the shirt over her head and deposited it on the floor by her feet. She removed her bra next, letting it land by her shirt. Her chest was exquisite, just a palmful really, but creamy soft skin, and pale pink nipples he hungered to taste.

'And now the skirt.'

Her fingers fumbled with the button, and once it was free, she began thrusting it down her hips.

'Slowly,' he whispered.

Savannah caught his eyes and her movements slowed. She carefully pushed the material over her bottom and down her legs, bending at the waist while her eyes watched his.

His lips separated and he sucked in a deep breath. 'Just like that, baby. Nice and slow. I've been waiting for this too long to rush through it.'

Once she was standing in front of him, dressed in just her panties, Cole drew her to his chest and held her there, her feminine form molding to his masculine one. He held her for moment, needing to feel the warmth of her skin pressed his against his, and the steady thump of her heartbeat against his chest. He tipped her chin up with one finger and bent to kiss her, to worship her mouth like she deserved. She parted her lips, accepting him, rubbing her tongue against his. The raw need in her kiss pushed him over the edge, and he pulled away, breathless.

'Undo my pants,' he growled between kisses.

Savannah looked down at his belt buckle like it was some foreign contraption. He lowered his head to kiss her again and felt her hands working to free the clasp, before moving on to the button on his jeans. With one hand cradling her jaw, his other reached down to assist, lowering his zipper, and pushing his jeans down his thighs. Savannah broke the kiss to look down, and he watched as she became acquainted with his erection for the first time. Still clad in black boxer briefs, he was barely contained, tenting the material rather impressively. Savannah reached down and, with a single fingertip, touched him. His dick jumped.

Her face awash with desire, she reached out to touch him again, gripping his length through the material.

Fuck. The grip of her tiny hand was a thing of magic. He fought with himself, locking his knees and struggling to keep himself in check. He wanted to yank the boxers down and let her explore, but his need to touch her first won out. He lifted her underneath her arms and placed her carefully on the bed. She let out a surprised gasp, but stayed put on the center of the bed.

Cole joined her, lying on his side. Filtered moonlight and the dim light from the hallway cast enough of a glow to watch each other. Really see each other for the first time. Knowing this moment was about to change everything between them, Cole took his time, forcing his heart rate to slow. He admired the beautiful girl in his bed. He'd spent every night with her for several weeks now, but he usually did his damnedest to avoid checking her out. Now, he didn't hold back. His eyes raked over her skin — the soft, lovely curves of her breasts, her smooth shoulders, and the dip in her stomach that led to shapely hips. Her eyes wandered his physique too, a little smile on her lips as she looked over his torso. She placed a single hand on the center of his stomach, letting it glide up and over his pecs, then down over his abs again — but not going any lower. He could see her pulse thrumming incessantly in her neck, practically hear her erratic heartbeat in the weighty silence of the room. But she didn't look afraid, more like curious about what would happen next.

Cole let her touch him, remaining still and silent. Chill bumps broke out over his skin as desire and need raced through his system. Her hand met the waistband of his boxers before skittering away to move back up his chest. Her palm settled over his heart, which was fucking pounding against his ribcage. She smiled softly at him, leaving her hand to rest there as if saying, it's okay, I feel it too.

He explored her body next. He'd resisted for too long. His fingertips traced her hip bone, her skin warm and incredibly soft. He trailed his index finger up the center of her stomach to the patch of skin between her breasts, wanting to take them in his hands, hell, wanting to take them in his mouth, but he paused, resting his palm against her chest. She met his eyes, seeking approval, seeking…assurance about how he felt. But rather than answer her unspoken question, about what this meant between them, he leaned over and pressed a soft kiss to her mouth. 'Are you sure?'

Her eyes flickered open, finding his. 'Yes.'

He remembered how responsive she'd been the one and only time he'd allowed himself to touch her, and couldn't wait to see her come undone again, to watch her back arch and hear her call his name. He lifted up on one elbow and kissed Savannah deeply, their mouths fused together in a hot mass of sliding wet tongues and lips seeking…always seeking. With his mouth firmly over hers, Cole's hand moved of its own accord, need spiking inside him strong and sure. He palmed her breasts, his thumb grazing her nipple. She inhaled sharply at the contact, but his hand continued its path south, not stopping until he was cupping the mound of sensitive flesh between her legs, his fingers pushing past her panties to brush lightly against her bare skin. Her mouth stilled on his, falling open when his fingers glided over the seam of her pussy, parting her to caress the sensitive nub. His fingers sought and rubbed, soft touches designed only to bring her pleasure. Her eyes remained on his, a little crease lining her forehead, like she was silently fighting with herself. Her body wanted this — she was already wet — but he could tell her mind was racing.

'Cole …' She gripped his wrist, preventing his hand from going any closer to the spot she wanted him.

'Savannah?' His voice was thick with desire. 'I'm sorry. I shouldn't have…Do you need me to stop?'

'Just give me a second…' She squeezed her eyes closed, needing to think. The first time he'd touched her, she was tipsy from the alcohol and so desperate for contact after watching the erotic scene with Sali. Jacob's gruff voice had been decidedly absent during her first encounter with Cole. But now, stone sober, with him looking at her like he wanted to eat her alive, his hot thick erection pressing against her hip, she needed a minute to gather her thoughts. Or more aptly, to turn off the unwelcome thoughts currently swirling inside her head.

He shifted on the bed, rising up on his elbow to look down at her. 'Tell me what you're thinking.' His features were washed in pale blue moonlight and his eyes were dark with concern.

She swallowed and let out a sigh. 'I don't know. Jacob always said that men wanted only one thing from a woman—the pleasures of the flesh. And once they had what they wanted, they left. They always left.' She twisted her hands in her lap, hating her nakedness in this moment, wishing she could draw the sheet up over her chest without seeming overly uptight. 'I want to…but I'm just…scared.'

He drew a deep breath, his chest lifting as his lungs expanded. 'You're afraid that's all I want from you? Or that I'll leave you after?'

'Both I guess…and if you don't want me here after this, I don't have enough for an apartment yet…'

'Savannah,' he groaned. 'This isn't all I want from you. I've been fighting myself constantly; I shouldn't want this at all. I convinced myself that all I wanted and needed from you was the chance to take care of you like you deserved. To keep you safe. To help you to be happy. And then you totally shocked me. You were confident and determined when most would have been terrified. You were teaching me. You refused to crumble; you have strength where I don't.'

'Of course that's not true. You're insanely strong,' she scoffed.

He glanced down and shook his head. 'I promise you I'm not. But we're getting off topic.' He clasped both of her hands between his. 'What Jacob told you was bullshit. Some men are assholes, sure, but not all. And you have way more to offer than that bastard gave you credit for.'

She twisted her hands together, trying to process his words. If she was being completely honest, she knew her fears were about more than just what Jacob had taught her. She'd witnessed Cole's track record with women, his casual attitude toward sex, and this wasn't just some physical act to her. It was so much more. 'It's not just what Jacob said…I've met some of the women you've slept with, Cole. I don't want to be part of that pattern.'

'I'm sorry, I'm not getting this right. I'm not good with feelings and declarations of emotion… but I want you here, Savannah. And we don't have to do…this. I just like having you with me. You smell nice. You cook for me, you hum when you carry Cuddles around the house — which is the worst name ever, by the way — and after having you live here with me, I'm terrified I won't be able to go back to living alone. So you better not go anywhere.'

She dared a glance at his eyes again. His brow was crinkled in concentration and his look was determined and sure. He was telling the truth. He felt something for her. Even if it wasn't love…she knew it was close. And she would take it. Take him and everything he had to offer her. Realizing that Jacob was wrong, at least about this one man made her chest tight. 'Cole.' The word broke across her lips. There were no words to describe how she felt in that moment.

'I'll always want you here. And it's not because of this…' He smoothed a hand across her naked physique, giving her a shoulder squeeze.

His words gave her the courage to continue. Jacob wouldn't rob her of this experience. She wouldn't let their pasts taint it. She couldn't summon the words to tell him what she wanted, but she knew she could show him. Savannah crawled on top of Cole, settling against the length of him. His arms automatically surrounded her, pulling her to his chest and rubbing her back. Savannah could feel his erection had softened, and she feared that the moment had passed. She didn't want to be responsible for ruining her first time. She angled her mouth up to meet his and pressed a soft kiss against his jaw, the corner of his mouth, his bottom lip. He responded slowly, carefully, tenderly kissing her back, but much more delicately than before. His fingers laced in her hair, his other hand cupped her jaw. She wanted to show him she was ready for more but didn't know what to do, how to recapture the moment. She separated his lips with her own and felt a low rumble in the back of his throat when their tongues met. She felt his manhood thicken and stir to life beneath the fabric of his boxers.

She broke the kiss, needing more, wanting to be closer. 'Cole?'

'Yeah babe?' His breathing was ragged, like he was doing everything in his power to let her go slow. Too bad she was done with slow. She bit her lip and reached a tentative hand between them as if seeking his permission. 'Savannah?'

'I want you…' she murmured lightly, raking her nails along his chest. 'I want to touch you.'

He groaned in relief and pushed his boxers down his hips. She moved next to him, allowing him to remove the last stitch of clothing between them. Her hand moved on its own, needing to touch the fine hair trailing down his lower stomach. His breath caught in his throat when her fingertips meant his skin and she smiled, liking the effect she had on him.

She reached lower, testing the weight of his thick length in her hand. 'Cole…show me…' She breathed against his mouth.

Her eyes locked on his. The mocha-colored depths that always held the promise of protection now swirled with something much more. The promise of complete and total sexual satisfaction. Savannah knew he would own her if he so chose. And she wanted nothing more. She wanted to loose herself in Cole, to experience everything she could. To enjoy this moment like it was her last.

He needed to feel the warmth of her hand against his skin before he came just thinking about it. He pressed a soft kiss to Savannah's mouth and reached for her hand. She carefully took his considerable length in her palm, as if unsure what to do with it.

'Touch me, baby,' he encouraged, guiding her hand down his manhood. He closed his fist around hers and demonstrated, drawing his hand up the length and squeezing over the head. A curse rumbled through his chest, breaking from his lips in a desperate cry.

Her hand stilled, and for a moment his own palm fluttered over hers, ready to encourage, to show her what he liked, but when he saw her uncertain gaze, he stopped himself and balled his fists at his sides instead. 'It's okay. You don't have to do anything you're not ready for.'

'It's not that.' She brought her index finger to him and rubbed the drop of warm fluid at the tip without knowing how amazing that simple touch felt to him. 'I want to taste you,' she murmured.

His heart kicked at her confession. The honest need in her voice was the most erotic thing Cole had ever heard. Would ever hear, he was certain. 'Fuck, Savannah.' She remained stock still, her eyes still on his. 'Sorry,' he muttered an apology for the curse. He never realized what a dirty mouth he had until Savannah arrived, but she didn't seem to mind.

'It's okay.' She smiled. She crawled down his body until she was face-to-face with his insanely hard cock jutting out in front of him, as if seeking out Savannah, begging for her attention. Determined green eyes met his. 'Tell me if I do something wrong.'

He doubted that'd be happening. She could practically look at his dick at this point and he'd love it. 'Don't worry about that.' She couldn't do anything wrong. Well, he supposed that wasn't entirely accurate. He considered warning her to be careful of her teeth, but decided against it. He'd gently correct her if it was an issue, but until then, he'd let her explore without any fear or self-consciousness.

Savannah sat back on her heels, lifted his cock away from his body and then lowered her head. With eyes locked on his, she planted a tender kiss against the head. He was already leaking pearly fluid, and his scrotum was drawn tight against his body. He was poised and ready to explode.

She took him into the depths of her warm mouth. His hips shot forward off the bed, but she welcomed the intrusion, suckling at his most sensitive skin. 'Fuck baby. Yeah. Just like that…' He stroked her jaw, pushed her hair back from her face, and palmed her cheek. He watched Savannah kiss and lick the length of him and was lost to the mind-numbing bliss of the moment.

She was so nurturing, so giving in everything she did, and pleasuring him was no exception. She left everything on the table, licking, kissing and stroking him as if her sole purpose was to please him.

Soon Savannah was clenching her thighs together and moaning for her own release, and he hadn't even touched her yet. He pulled himself free from Savannah's mouth and hauled her up his body. 'My turn,' he explained at the surprise on her face.

Cole settled her against the pillow so she was lying next to him. He dropped a kiss to her lips, then slid his middle finger into her mouth, wetting it. She drew the digit in without question, swirling her tongue against his skin.

'We need to make sure you're ready for me,' he explained.

She looked down at his long cock, resting heavily against her hip and then back up at him. 'Will it hurt?'

'At first, yes But I'll do my best to go slow.'

She nodded, trusting him.

When his finger slid inside her slowly, carefully, Savannah's mouth dropped open. And when he drew it back and began fucking her with his hand, just a little faster with each stroke, Savannah's knees fall apart and dropped her head back against the pillow. His other hand joined the fun, rubbing slow circles against her flesh, unwilling to rush her. Soon she was soaking wet and moaning his name, and seconds later, with her head thrown back in ecstasy, she came for him. Cole planted wet kisses all along her throat, refusing to ease up until he'd milked every last ounce of pleasure from her.

After several minutes of nuzzling against her neck, and kissing her through all the small aftershocks of her release, Savannah crawled on his lap to straddle him, placing a knee on either side of his thighs.

'Cole?'

He didn't respond. He knew what she was asking for, and unable to deny her, he reached for the side table and grabbed a condom. She watched as he put it on, her gaze flickering back and forth between his eyes and his manhood. He could read her expression as if she'd written it out. She was trying to understand where exactly he was going to fit that.

'Savannah, we don't have to.'

Her eyes captured his. 'I want to.' She planted her palms on his tense stomach muscles, and lifted herself up, trying to find the right angle.

'Come here.' Cole pulled her down onto his chest, needing to kiss her. He planted sweet kisses along her mouth and throat. He understood the gravity of this moment, of what she was giving him, and he wouldn't rush it. Not when they were so close. She deserved to be worshipped and taken care of her first time. He would do everything in his power to make it what she deserved. 'Just relax, babe. Let me.' Savannah relaxed in his arms, and Cole kissed her deeply as he reached behind her, holding himself in place until Savannah began to ease back, taking him in.

She ran her hands over his chest and closed her eyes, a look of concentration settling over her features. Then she eased down on him, lowering her hips so he sunk inside her in mind-blowing slowness. Blinding pleasure rocketed through him. Fuck, she was tight. She rocked against him, pulling him deeper in tiny increments.

'Shit….' He bit back a groan.

Savannah's eyes widened and found his, blinking down at him. Damn she looked so innocent, he almost questioned what he was doing. Almost. But they'd gone too far to turn back now. He was inside her sweet pink pussy, slick with moisture and heat. He wouldn't talk her out of this, not now.

'Everything okay?' he asked instead, needing to hear her say it was all right to continue.

She nodded, and leaned forward to kiss him, gliding her tongue against his. Pleasure shot straight to his balls, drawing them up close to his body. He held her close and punctuated each kiss by lifting his hips to ease deeper inside her.

Her soft grunts and groans matched his thrusts, eating away at his self-control. He knew he wouldn't last long.

'Does it feel good?' he asked, slowing his pace.

Savannah opened her eyes, her bright green gaze blinking at him in wonder. 'Yeah.'

Her cheeks were flushed pink and he couldn't resist watching her enjoyment. She'd stopped moving against him and allowed him to hold her hips while he thrust up into her. Sex was a physical act, so why should he feel more? But he couldn't deny that he'd never felt closer to anyone. Savannah broke through all his barriers. She was needy, yet giving, sensual yet innocent, trusting and timid. She'd put both their pleasure, the whole experience, in his hands and the gravity of the moment was not lost on him.

He slid in again, exquisitely slowly until he was buried deep again. Her breath hitched, catching in her throat.

'Does it hurt?'

'Only a little.'

Damn, he was hoping it didn't, but it was to be expected. It was her first time after all. 'Do you want me to come?' he breathed against her mouth.

'Yes.'

He pulled out and situated her so she was lying back against the pillows. He preferred being on top — being the one in control—and it was a sure fire way to get him to come quickly. He gripped her hips, his fingers clutching to pull her towards him with each thrust.

Her groans grew louder, less contained, and Cole found himself being more vocal than usual. 'God you're beautiful…' A few more thrusts. 'Oh fuck…'

His hand snaked between them to bring her pleasure, rubbing, circling, using their moisture to send her over the edge again, and watching her come apart again sent him tumbling along after her, cursing and gasping as her tight channel milked him dry.

Chapter 25

Savannah and Cole had fallen asleep cuddled together, exhausted and spent after their love making the night before.

Cole stretched his arms over his head, his neck cracking with the effort. Savannah mumbled something in her sleep and then rolled over to find him, drawing her body tightly against his. He smoothed a hand along her hip, pulling her even closer. He was glad to see that in the sober, stark morning light, things didn't feel awkward between them. It was the opposite, in fact. This felt incredibly natural.

Savannah sleepily smiled and nuzzled against his neck. 'Morning,' she breathed against his skin.

'Morning.' He was suddenly aware that she was wearing one of his T-shirts with nothing on underneath, and that he had slept nude for the first time since Savannah had moved in. Memories of the previous night played at the edges of his mind, Savannah's determination to please him, her tiny whimpers and flushed pink skin, the way she gripped his biceps when he sank into her. His cock stirred to life.

He traced a fingertip over her hip, pushing the T-shirt up and out of his way. Savannah trembled as the pad of his finger slowly caressed her. His hand moved down to cup her pubic bone, and she let out a groan. He rolled over, so they were facing each other in the center of the bed, the covers strewn about them, providing a warm cocoon.

He lowered his mouth to hers, kissing her softly at first. Savannah, ever responsive, moaned quietly against his lips. She draped her leg across his waist, and pulled herself in tighter against his body.

'You're not too sore, are you?'

'I don't think so.'

She hadn't been up and out of bed yet either, but Cole nodded. 'Good.' His hand found his cock and he stroked it slowly, bumping against her thigh with each stroke. Savannah's eyes widened and then cast down to watch his movements. She bit her lip and whimpered, her hands scrambling to join his.

Once her warm hands were stroking him, Cole brought his hands to Savannah's face. He held her jaw and kissed her deeply, sucking her tongue into his mouth.

A sound from beyond his bedroom door captured their attention and they broke apart, breathing raggedly.

'What the fuck?' he muttered. 'Wait here.' He sprang from the bed and pulled on a pair of pajama pants before going to investigate.

Marissa was in his kitchen, fumbling with the coffee maker.

'What are you doing here?' He fumbled to tie the string on his waistband, panic rising that Marissa would know he'd slept with Savannah. But unless she'd checked the guest room and found it empty, maybe their secret was still safe.

She set the coffee to brew and turned to face him. 'Liam and I both crashed here last night. Hope that's okay. We were too tanked to drive.'

He swung around to the living room and found Liam still sleeping on his couch. *Where had Marissa slept?*

'We both just crashed on the couch. It was no big deal.'

Marissa didn't know. Relief flooded his system. He didn't even process that Liam and his sister shared a couch.

'Yeah, no problem.' He ran a hand across his hair in an attempt to smooth it down.

Savannah emerged from the bedroom, dressed in jeans and one of his sweatshirts that hung nearly to her knees.

'I was cold,' she explained at his and Marissa's stares. Cole studied her for clues about how she felt about last night. He couldn't believe he'd allowed things to go as far as they did. But Savannah's smile as she flitted past him and into the kitchen calmed him ever-so-slightly. If she didn't regret it, he wouldn't either. Plus it was hard to regret the best sex of his life.

Cole escaped the kitchen, needing a cold shower and time to collect his thoughts.

He returned fifteen minutes later, no further along in understanding what was happening between him and Savannah. The scent of bacon frying quieted his worries for the moment.

As usual, Savannah had cooked enough to feed twenty people. She still didn't have portion control mastered, having cooked for an entire compound of people in her past life. She arranged a platter of homemade blueberry muffins, a warming tray containing scrambled eggs, and a plate piled with crisp bacon on the center island, before turning to pour Cole's coffee.

Cole's gaze flashed to Marissa. Her eyes followed Savannah's movements, watching her fuss over Cole, adding milk to his coffee, and setting his iPad on the counter next to him. And she'd been watching too when Cole had run point on morning duty, taking Cuddles outside to do her business, and then adding a scoop of food to her bowl in the kitchen. They moved about each other effortlessly, yet with obvious care and reverence.

'Cole, can I have a word?' Marissa asked.

He glanced up from his iPad, a strip of bacon halfway to his mouth, and sighed. 'Sure.' His eyes travelled between Marissa and Liam's form, stretched out on his couch, looking damn smug. He'd need to get to the bottom of that later. His sister was off-fucking-limits and Liam should have known better. But Cole stood and followed Marissa into the laundry off the kitchen. She slid the pocket door closed behind them.

'Do I want to know what happened between you and Liam last night?'

Her lips twitched as she fought a smile. 'Probably not.'

'Fuck Rissa.' He crossed his arms over his chest and glared. 'That's not what I brought you in here to discuss.' Her hands flew to her hips. 'I want to talk about what's going on between you and Savannah.'

He shook his head. He wouldn't go there with Marissa. He wouldn't even go there in his own mind, and there was no point in talking about something he didn't even understand. 'Nothing to talk about. She needed a place to stay — I gave her one. You already know that. End of story.'

'Cole, you've never been good at relationships.'

'Exactly. So when are you going to stop trying to set me up?'

She shook her head. 'That's not what I'm talking about.'

He waited impatiently, tapping a bare foot against the wood floor.

'You can't deny that you're different with Savannah. You're in tune with her emotions, her needs. I've never seen you like this.'

He opened his mouth to respond, but found himself speechless. He couldn't deny he was in tune with Savannah; he knew her body's yearnings, read her emotions better than his own. But it was only because she was in his care, and he took that responsibility seriously. Perhaps he'd softened these past few years watching his friends get married and have babies. And then having Savannah in his life had pushed him over the edge. He drew a deep breath. 'Listen, Savannah has a job now, and she's saving up for her own apartment. I'm helping her out, sure, but this is a temporary situation between us.' Even as he said the words, part of him hoped they weren't true.

Marissa frowned and shook her head. 'That's what I was afraid of.' She patted his chest. 'You, my brother, are an idiot.'

Cole remained speechless in the center of the laundry room as Marissa opened the door and strolled away. He shook his head and followed her back to the kitchen.

Chapter 26

Cole had gotten rid of Marissa and Liam after breakfast, then he'd carried Savannah back to bed. She had begged him to let her shower first, and he'd finally released her. 'Try and make it a quick one.'

As she stood in front of the large mirror waiting for the water to heat, Savannah looked at the nude reflection before her. Her chest was high and perky, her stomach soft, but mostly flat, her thighs a bit bigger than she would have liked, but she couldn't deny that for the first time — maybe ever — she felt beautiful.

Whenever Cole looked at her, a certain flush caused her cheeks to glow, her stomach to flutter, and she felt completely wanted and desirable. But last night was the first time he'd acted on the desire she'd sensed burned inside him too. She was happy and relieved to see that the harsh light of morning, and Marissa's pointed stares, hadn't done anything to dampen his interest. As soon as the front door had closed on their overnight guests, Cole had pulled her mouth to his, his hands settling on her hips. They'd kissed softly, deeply, unlike the frenzied storm of last night, while he walked her backwards down the hallway towards his bedroom. Then he'd lifted her as though she weighed nothing at all and placed her carefully in the center of the bed and just looked at her.

Savannah tucked away the memory of hunger burning in his dark gaze and stepped under the stream of water.

The blissfully hot spray cascaded down her body and, even though she wanted to stand there and enjoy the warmth, she found herself rushing, if only to get back Cole a little quicker. She lathered her hair with the pink grapefruit shampoo and then tipped her head to rinse the suds. After working the conditioner through her long strands, she stepped out of the direct spray of the water to soap up her body from head to toe. Once she was sure she was clean, she rinsed her hair and shut off the water. It was only then she noticed a large form on the other side of the glass. Her heart flew into her throat. 'Cole!' She grabbed a towel from the hook and quickly wrapped it around herself. 'You scared me. How long were you watching me?'

He looked down sheepishly. Savannah's gaze followed his. *Oh my.* His large erection pressed against the thin cotton pants. 'Long enough,' he muttered, his voice thick.

She smiled and her heart began to slow. She grabbed a second towel to wrap around her dripping hair.

'I'm just going to jump in quick.' Cole gave her a kiss and then stepped out of his pajama pants and into the shower.

The idea of watching Cole shower was more appealing than going to get dressed, and she stood there momentarily distracted by the streams of water running down his lean body, over the lines of his six-pack abs, and she shivered. Her gaze wandered lower. He was still half-hard and she felt herself growing warm all over.

Wanting to step under the water with him, she made herself flee the bathroom and darted to the guest room. She dressed in panties and a tank top and partially dried her hair so it didn't turn into a crazy frizzy mess. Then she waited for him in his bed.

She pulled the sheets around her body and snuggled in to his pillow, inhaling his scent with each breath. Cole emerged a few minutes later, his skin still damp and glistening with tiny droplets of water, and a white towel fastened around his hips.

'You better not have gotten dressed under there,' he whispered, leaning down to plant a kiss on her mouth.

She swallowed. 'You'll just have to come find out.' If this is what flirting was like, sign her up. Cole made her feel alive and deliriously happy, like all her senses were heightened and she would never stop smiling. But she didn't have much time to examine her feelings, because he let the towel drop from his hips and stood before her, fully hard and insanely hot. Savannah gave in, throwing back the blankets and crawling across the bed until she was face to face with his manhood. Kneeling on all fours, she aligned her mouth with his waiting cock. He looked down and stroked her jaw. Savannah placed sweet kisses along the head and shaft, but when her tongue darted out to taste the tip, his hips jerked forward and he let out a groan. Enjoying having him completely at her mercy, Savannah wrapped a hand around his base and slipped her mouth around him, sliding back and forth.

He cursed and buried his hands in her hair. She began losing herself in his pleasure, rocking her hips and adding little moans of her own.

Cole's hand moved from her hair, trailing down her back and cupped her ass. His fingers found their way inside her panties to her damp center. He massaged that spot he seemed to instinctually know brought her pleasure. She gasped and rocked against his hand, while continuing to pleasure him with her mouth.

Savannah was soon soaking wet and ready, and Cole's firm hand on her jaw brought her back to reality, if only for a second. She lifted her eyes to his, her mouth still full of him. 'Fuck, that's a pretty sight.' He stroked her cheek with his thumb, and watched in reverence as she continued her slow, steady movements. The desire etched into his features was about to undo her.

Cole suddenly lifted her, situating her so she was on her back so fast she wasn't even sure what had happened. He peeled off her panties and then he was on top of her, pushing her tank top up to kiss her breasts.

'Are you sure you're not too sore?' His eyes flicked up to hers while he planted damp kisses all along her chest and in between her breasts.

She knew what she wanted, and it wasn't to discuss *that*. She wrapped a leg around his hip, pulling him in closer. 'Cole. Condom. Now.'

He chuckled against her throat and released her only long enough to fumble at the nightstand. She heard the sound of a package crinkling and then he was back to kissing her. Their mouths moved together in a frantic collision of gliding tongues and subtle moans.

Cole lifted himself off of her just enough to reach between them. His eyes stayed locked on hers as he positioned himself at her entrance and gently pushed forward. She wrapped both legs around his back, locking her ankles and angled up to meet his careful thrusts.

He planted a soft kiss on her mouth and pushed forward again, slipping inside her in a blinding sensation of heat and fullness. Her back arched from the bed and he tucked his face in against her throat, kissing and murmuring sweet things … how good she felt … how beautiful she was.

Savannah squeezed her eyes closed and matched his pace, forcing her hips up off the bed to angle towards his.

His mouth was everywhere—near her ear so she could hear his throaty gasps, on her neck, kissing and nibbling against her tender flesh, covering hers in a scorching hot kiss. She writhed underneath him, heading closer and closer to ecstasy with every brutal thrust, each sweet kiss. 'Cole,' she moaned, lifting her hips to his one final time as wave after wave of pleasure rocketed through her core.

He slowed his pace, seeming to understand her need to ride out the intense burst of pleasure for as long as she possibly could.

She released a final groan and scraped her nails down his back as she grasped at something to hold onto, something to ground her.

Cole took her hands, pinning them above her head and increased his rhythm, pounding into her at a steady pace until she felt his entire body stiffen and jerk, and she knew he had found his release, too.

He collapsed next to her in a heap, pulling her body to his so that her back was pressed to his front. He draped a heavy arm around her waist, anchoring her to his chest. Savannah closed her eyes and released a soft sigh, feeling safe and happier than she ever remembered.

Chapter 27

Cole's phone chimed with a new message. He untangled his arm from around Savannah and punched in his security code to unlock it. Shit. It was a text from Sali.

Up for hanging out later?

Savannah lifted her head from his chest and he dropped the phone onto the coffee table in front of them. When he dared a glance down at Savannah, he could have sworn he saw tears swimming in her eyes, but she blinked and the effect was gone, making him wonder if he'd only imagined the tears. They'd been in a state of bliss for weeks—having regular sex and sleeping together in Cole's bed every night. Damned if he'd let Sali ruin it.

He cupped her cheek in his palm. 'Hey, I'm staying in tonight. Just you and me.'

She managed a smile and he leaned in to kiss her. 'Okay,' she breathed.

He guided her head back to its spot in the crook between his shoulder and neck. Sali had texted him a few times over the past couple of weeks, and he'd tried to let her down gently, but apparently it was time for brutal honesty. He wasn't interested. But he didn't want to respond right now. Seeing the hurt in Savannah's eyes was too much.

He still didn't know what this thing was with Savannah, but he knew these past few weeks with her had changed him. She'd given herself up so willingly; she was so vulnerable and giving, it tore him open. He was just waiting for her to see through him. There were times when she looked at him, really looked at him, and he wondered if she saw his need to keep everyone at arm's length, unable to love after so much loss. They had yet to have any sort of relationship discussion, but Cole had no intentions of dating anyone else right now. And though his head continued to be at war with his heart, he justified his relationship with Abbie. It wasn't really cheating since he wasn't sleeping with her. Was it? Fuck.

He knew Savannah was too young for him, that she'd need to spread her wings and explore, but for now, he was happy that he was part of the growth. And more than that, when he got too close, he hurt people. Abbie was the perfect example of that. He couldn't live with himself if he did to Savannah what he did to Abbie. He would do everything in his power to shield Savannah from his past, even if it meant concealing the truth from her. For now. He also didn't know how Abbie would react to him having someone else in his life, and he wasn't looking forward to having that particular conversation. When had his life gotten so complicated?

He pulled Savannah closer and tried to push everything else from his mind. Lingering fears over that weirdo Dillon kept him on edge, but Savannah's sweet presence in his life eased some of his tension. He didn't want to worry just now. He smoothed a hand over Savannah's arms, caressing her lightly. He would handle it and keep her safe one way or another. He had to.

'Cole?' She lifted her head.

'Hmm.' He absently trailed his fingers along her arm.

'Can I ask you something?'

The hair on the back of his neck rose. *Crap.* He knew that this conversation was going to be about more than which movie to watch next. 'Of course.'

'What's going to happen to us?'

He hadn't been prepared for question. Though any other topic was fair game between them, they'd refused to talk about the future, sticking to topics no further ahead than what to do for dinner, next weekend's plans, or at the furthest—when Cuddles' next set of puppy shots were due. They'd existed in their own little bubble, taking pleasure from each other's bodies and living comfortably together. But Savannah's whispered conversations on the phone with Marissa about apartment décor were not lost on him. He wondered if she was still planning on moving out, despite the intimacy of their new relationship. Which was for the best, he told himself. He had no delusions of true love, soul mates, marriage or kids. It was easier, and a hell of a lot safer, to be on his own. He couldn't accept just yet that Savannah might be the one to change his mind.

'What do you mean?' he asked, stalling for more time.

'I just wonder sometimes what you…want.' Her expression was so open, so honest, he could read her like a book

He turned to face her, holding her jaw in his hand. 'I'm not going anywhere, Savannah.' He pressed a soft kiss to her mouth. He knew it wasn't exactly the declaration of love and commitment she probably wanted, but it was as close as he could get. There was still too much she didn't know about him, too much she wouldn't understand. This is what he had to offer — protection, devotion and mind-blowing sex. He hoped it was enough. Because, damn it, he couldn't offer her more. Not with his spectacular track record for botching the shit out of relationships.

She nodded, seeming to accept his non answer, and leaned in for another kiss. If the physical was all they would share, neither of them seemed willing to squander it. Their kisses turned heated, and he pulled her into his lap, his mouth moving down her throat as her hands worked their way under his shirt, tenderly massaging the muscles in his back and reaching around him to run along his tense abs. He yanked his shirt off over his head and her shirt and bra soon followed, landing on the floor between the couch and coffee table. She rocked her hips against his, discovering he was already hard. Watching her confidence grow, seeing the look of desire reflected in her eyes, sparked his own need. He gripped her arms, pinning them to her sides. He'd discovered that just as much as he liked taking charge, Savannah enjoyed being man-handled. She folded her arms behind her back, interlaced her fingers and thrust her chest out. He held her hands with one of his and worked his other into the front of her jeans. He feasted on the warm tip of each breast until Savannah was crying out and had worked her hands free to tug on his hair.

Cole shifted her on his lap — providing just enough room between them to undo his jeans and free himself. Savannah crouched in front of him and peeled off her jeans. Cole assisted, tugging the material down her legs until she could kick the jeans to the floor. She watched as he made quick work of putting on a condom, then sunk down onto him without hesitation, surrendering as he filled her.

'God, you're tight.' He pressed a kiss to her mouth. She gripped his shoulders, her nails biting into his skin, and began to rock against him.

Watching her move above him, testing and finding her rhythm, was the hottest thing he could've ever imagined. Her tight body riding his was too much. His head dropped back against the sofa and his eyes drifted closed. She placed a palm on either side of his face and he opened his eyes. She leaned in to kiss him, their tongues colliding and breaths mingling.

'Cole…' she grunted, bracing her hands on his thighs as she lifted up and down.

'You feel too damn good. How is this even possible?' 'Because it's us,' she said simply.

He believed her assessment. Wholeheartedly. But wouldn't deny the fact that scared the shit out of him. He had never known a better lover, which made no sense, considering Savannah's lack of experience. Their bodies fit together like two halves. There hadn't been any hint of a fumbling, awkward stage like he'd known with previous lovers. Their bodies were so in-sync, they seemed to anticipate each other's movements and respond in turn, bringing pleasure that he hadn't known could exist before Savannah.

Her flesh gripped him from the inside out, and he felt her begin to tremble. She rode him fast and hard as she reached climaxed, whimpering a series of tiny moans then fell forward onto his chest, completely spent. Watching Savannah orgasm quickly brought him to his own climax. She no longer seemed capable of moving against him; he gripped her waist and lifted her up and down on him a few final times until he followed her over the edge.

Chapter 28

Cole shoved his feet into his shoes and wandered to the kitchen. 'I have to go out for a little bit.' He rested a hand on her hip and leaned in for a kiss.

Her eyes flew to the clock on the stove. He knew that his Sunday appointments were becoming a point of contention in their relationship and a source of burning curiosity for Savannah. She opened her mouth, the question right there on her tongue, but paused. What would he say if she finally had the courage to ask? She closed her mouth and nodded. 'Okay.'

He left a few minutes later. He was tired of feeling like he practically needed to sneak out of his own house on Sunday afternoons. He hated the guilty feeling that followed him as he drove. He didn't like leaving Savannah. He didn't like that he had to do this. But this was what needed to be done if he wanted to right his past wrongs. And he owed her this much — one hour of his time. And he knew Savannah would never understand it.

Savannah dutifully followed Marissa from store to store, until her back ached and her arms quivered from carrying all the shopping bags. They ended up at Liam's pub for a drink. Liam poured them each a glass of chilled white wine and set a bowl of salted almonds in front of them. Savannah noticed his eyes strayed to Marissa's every few minutes, regardless of who he was serving at the bar.

Savannah took a sip of her wine. *Mmm.* Sweet notes of pear and a crisp apricot finish met her tongue. Her mind wandered for the hundredth time to Cole and his hasty departures on Sundays. She considered asking Marissa about it, but decided against it since she wasn't sure she could handle the information. 'Can I ask you about Cole?' Savannah bit her lip, the butterflies taking flight inside her.

'Sure.' Marissa shrugged, popping an almond into her mouth.

'Cole's sort of…' She frowned struggling for the right words. Hard to get to know? Closed off?

'Emotionally stunted?' Marissa offered.

Savannah exhaled, a breathy little laugh escaping. 'Yes.'

Marissa nodded and smiled weakly. 'You care for him.'

It wasn't a question so Savannah didn't bother to answer. Was it that obvious?

Marissa contemplated the contents of her wine glass, twirling the stem in her hands. 'There's something I want to tell you.'

The feeling that the next few minutes were going to change things considerably pulsed low in Savannah's stomach.

Marissa confirmed that several months ago, Cole confided in her about his night terrors. He wouldn't talk about it for the longest time, but Marissa was unrelenting after he began losing weight and dark circles etched themselves under his eyes. He'd confided in Marissa about a case where an innocent girl was caught in the crossfire and ended up taking a bullet before he could take the suspect down. Marissa forced him to go to a doctor; he got on prescription anti-anxiety medication and sleeping pills that he took for months after her death. But he never really properly dealt with things, or accepted that her death wasn't his fault.

'But they were never involved…romantically?'

'No. They'd literally just met. Cole was there when she died and he blamed himself that he couldn't protect her.'

Stunned into silence, Savannah nodded. He was rehabilitating her, not because he had feelings for her, but because of his guilt over another girl's death.

'Are you okay? You're pale,' Marissa said.

Savannah's ears thundered with the sudden rush of blood, but she managed a nod. 'I'm fine. I just didn't know.'

Marissa patted her knee. 'I figured as much.' Marissa polished off the rest of her wine, and waved Liam off at his offer of a refill. 'My brother's falling for you. He just doesn't know it yet. Be patient with him, okay?'

Savannah nodded, her mouth dry and her stomach turning somersaults. 'Can we go?' She knew Cole would be back from whatever it was he did on Sundays and they needed to talk.

Marissa nodded, left a large tip for Liam, then drove her home.

After wrestling in shopping bags of clothes she no longer even remembered buying, Savannah scooped Cuddles up into her arms and headed outside, not quite ready to face Cole. When she reentered the apartment, she found him in the kitchen, digging through the take-out menus. 'Hey, I didn't know when you'd be home, so I figured I'd order out tonight.'

Savannah released a squirming Cuddles to the floor and stared at her feet.

'What's wrong?'

Hot, salty tears stung her eyes. 'We need to talk.'

Chapter 29

The single tear rolling down Savannah's cheek held him immobile for a moment. 'Savannah?' He stepped in closer, guiding her by the elbow towards the sofa. 'Tell me what happened.'

She fell to the couch, curled her legs under her, and let out a deep sigh. 'I talked to Marissa today.'

'Okay…' He braced himself, unsure what was coming.

'She told me about the girl…that passed away.'

'Oh.' Cole feared it was something far worse, something he'd kept buried away from everyone. But even as his pulse spiked, he knew it couldn't be. Because that was something not even Marissa knew. And he hoped she never would.

In a shaky voice, Savannah admitted to Cole that she feared it meant what was between them wasn't real.

He'd never considered the connection, but when confronted with the information — the link was obvious. Of course what he felt for Savannah was in a whole other league, his feelings for her much more intense. Christ, he'd been sharing his home with her for months now.

'That's all I was to you? Someone to save since you couldn't save the last girl?' The tears flowed freely, and she curled into herself, hugging her knees to her chest.

'Savannah…that's not…'

'I needed saving at one time, but not anymore…not now. Now I just need…' She paused, breather breathing shaky.

'Tell me.' He pulled her closer, forcing her to disentangle from her perch on the couch.

'To be loved. To be accepted.'

The deep knot that had been sitting inside his chest broke, and he drew a deep breath as though it was his first. His resolve broke away and he pulled Savannah to his chest. 'Shh. It's going to be okay. I promise you, you're so much more to me than a lost girl to save. Maybe that's all this was at the beginning, but not now.' It was the most he could give her. He couldn't promise her a future or unending love and devotion. His heart was little more than a scrap of flesh in his chest. It had been obliterated and smashed into tiny pieces one too many times. And his dirty little secret — the reason he left every Sunday—was going to be the final straw that drove her away. If they declared their love for each other, it would only make their eventual falling out that much worse.

Savannah's hot tears dampened his neck and ate away at his control. She pulled in a shaky breath at an attempt at getting her emotions under control.

'Cole. That wasn't your fault. You need to move past it. Overcome this fear of losing someone because you couldn't save that girl.'

A timid frown pulled at his lips. He hated how she looked at him. Like he was the one who was damaged. 'God, Savannah, you should be with someone who teaches you how to live life, not someone who's scared to live it, too.'

'So we'll teach each other. We'll take things one day at a time, be there, discover new passions and dreams together. We'll hold each other at night when the fears try to creep back in.'

He looked at her with anguish. If he could give her the world, he would. But he wouldn't have her settle. Not for him. Not when she deserved so much more. He didn't think there was ever two people better suited for each other, but something inside him seized up and he couldn't say the words. He couldn't tell her everything would be okay, he couldn't promise her forever. Not with all his baggage.

Silent tears streamed down her cheeks, and Cole wiped them away. 'Don't cry. I've got you. I'm right here.' He rubbed her back, and she let the tears come. Cole continued rubbing her back, murmuring soothing endearments near her ear, and most of all, he just held her and let her break down. He felt sure that her collapse was more than just from the information Marissa had shared with her. He'd been waiting for everything to hit her for some time now. And it seemed it finally had. Eventually her sobs quieted into little hiccups and Cole urged her from the crook of his neck that she'd claimed as her own.

She covered her face with her hands. 'Don't look at me. I'm hideous.'

He chuckled and removed her hands. 'You're not hideous.' Her eyes were swollen and red, her skin splotchy. 'You need a tissue, maybe, but you could never be hideous.'

She smiled and playfully swatted his hands away. 'I'm sorry I'm such a girl.'

He leaned forward and kissed her forehead. 'Never apologize for that, babe. Trust me, I'm very glad you're a girl.' He wiped his thumbs underneath her eyes, capturing some of the black mascara pooled there. 'Go get in bed. I'll get the tissues.'

She nodded and headed off down the hall.

Cole joined her in bed, his hands full with Cuddles tucked under one arm and a box of Kleenex in the other. 'Special delivery.' He smiled, placing the over-excited puppy on the bed. She quickly bounded over to Savannah and began licking her face.

Savannah giggled and set the puppy on her chest, patting her back. 'Thanks.'

Cole tucked the blankets around her. 'Just get some rest, and I'll take care of ordering dinner. Any special requests?'

She shook her head. 'Anything is fine. But no pizza. Oh, and maybe some dessert.'

He chuckled. 'Anything, as long as it's not pizza and includes dessert. You got it.' He turned off the lights and left, the heavy feeling once again settling inside his chest. Seeing her reaction tonight brought resounding clarity to his Sunday excursions—he could never ever tell her about Abbie. It would break her.

The following morning Cole laced up his running shoes. On his way to the running trails, he passed by his SUV and caught sight of s a white piece of paper tucked under his wiper blade.

A sinking feeling in his gut told him this wasn't an advertisement like solicitors sometimes left, blanketing all the cars. His training kicked in. He glanced around at his surroundings, but nothing was out of the ordinary. He plucked the scrap of paper and unfolded it.

You took something of mine and I will be back for her.

Fuck. Shivers crawled up his spine and his muscles tensed. He had been fearing for weeks that Dillon would reappear. He pocketed the paper and tore back up the stairs toward Savannah.

He kicked off his running shoes in the foyer, thankful that Savannah liked to sleep in on Sunday mornings. He debated what he would tell her when she woke. At least the building required a key to enter. He ran a hand through his hair. He didn't want to alarm Savannah, but was it even safe for her to go to work tomorrow? He paced the kitchen to avoid punching the wall. He needed to get his shit together and have his game face on by the time she woke up. He pressed the heel of his hand against his heart. Fucking chest was tight again.

He made a cup of coffee and brought it to the breakfast bar with trembling hands. He was too keyed up to sit, so he stood there, sucking down sips of the too hot coffee. He wouldn't tell Savannah. Not yet. Tomorrow he would go to work, gather anything he could find on Dillon, and he'd have Savannah do the same. He'd escort her to her car, send her to work like normal and then set about tracking this asshole down.

Chapter 30

The week passed without another note or any sign that Dillon had been back, but Cole's sense of panic hadn't subsided. Not at all. He still hadn't said anything to Savannah, but was more vigilant than ever — escorting her to her car, calling to check on her at work, insisting on taking Cuddles outside himself. He was beginning to suspect that she knew something was up, but it was almost as if she didn't want to know what — refusing to ask any questions, and instead let him be the overprotective alpha male he needed to be.

Searching the database at the Bureau hadn't turned up much, and he'd debated with himself all week about getting the police involved, and maybe even his boss Norm. If he did, he knew he'd have a lot of explaining to do about why a cult escapee was living in his home. He also knew that there was little the police could do with a vague handwritten note and only a gut feeling about who wrote it.

So instead he was extra diligent and watchful and kept Savannah close — the best he could do under the circumstances.

But Friday night when he got home from work and found another note — this time left at his front door — his passive-aggressive mode of dealing with this was over. The bastard had somehow breached the building security and delivered the note directly to his door. What if Savannah had been home? What if she'd let him in? And the messy text scrawled along the paper sent his heart racing into a murderous rage.

You took my heart. Now I'll take hers.

He called Savannah and found she was on her way home from work. He placed his handgun in the back of his jeans, locked the door behind him and went to wait for her in the parking lot. She smiled when she saw him and jogged from her car over to his side. But her smile fell when she took in the tense set of his shoulders and the frown tugging at his mouth. 'Cole?'

He dropped a kiss to her mouth and pulled her close. 'Come on, let's get inside.'

She allowed herself to be towed along beside him in jerking steps as he glanced at their surroundings.

Once inside, he pointed to the note on the island. 'Do you recognize that handwriting?'

Her concerned gaze met his and she crossed the room carefully, as if there was a live tiger in the kitchen rather than a scrap of paper. She reached for the paper, and Cole grabbed her wrist. 'No fingerprints,' he warned.

She nodded and leaned over the counter to read it. Her hand flew to her mouth. 'Where did you get this?'

'It was stuffed into the crack of the front door.'

All the color drained from her face and Cole's hands on her waist were the only thing keeping her on her feet.

'Do you know who it might be from?' He probed, wanting her honest assessment on the matter without his suspicions coloring her view.

'It's from Dillon.' Her voice was certain and sure. 'He used to always say that I'd captured his heart. And it looks like his handwriting too.' She turned into his chest, burying her face.

Cole's arms circled around her back, holding her close. 'We're going to get out of here for the weekend. Go stay somewhere else while I figure this out. I don't like that he knows where we are.'

Savannah nodded. 'Okay.'

He gave her a quick kiss. 'Go pack a bag. Be quick.'

'What about Cuddles?'

Shit. Damn dog. He considered dropping the thing off at Marissa's, but if by some chance Dillon was tracking their movements, he didn't want his sister involved. 'We'll see if Levi and Deb can take her for the weekend.'

He threw some clothes into a duffle bag, added his gun and an extra clip, then met Savannah in the kitchen where she was pouring dry dog food into a plastic bag. He threw their bags over his shoulder and they ventured down the hall towards Levi's unit with a carefree puppy jogging beside them.

When Deb answered the door, Cuddles charged past them. 'Sorry about that. Cuddles!' Savannah called after the naughty animal.

'Oh, that's okay. What's up?' Deb eyed the bags slung over Cole's shoulder.

He placed an arm around Savannah's waist and tugged her closer. 'We're going away for the weekend. Would you mind watching the dog for a couple of days?'

Deb's mouth curved in a grin. 'I knew there was something between you two. Sure. Why not?'

Savannah handed Deb the bag of food, Cuddles' favorite toy, and supplied her with instructions as well as the dog's likes and dislikes. A few minutes later, they were pulling away in his SUV, Cole watching the rearview mirror constantly until he was sure they weren't being followed. Savannah reached over and found his hand. His death grip on the steering wheel let up just slightly.

'I'm sorry,' she murmured.

'For what?'

'For unleashing this craziness on you…I doubt you wanted to spend your weekend on the run with me.'

He squeezed her hand, running his thumb across her knuckles. 'This isn't your fault. I don't want you to worry about anything.

I'm going to take care of this. I promise. And I meant what I told Deb. You and I are going to enjoy a romantic weekend getaway. That is…if you're game?'

She released a sigh. 'You mean, like pretend all this isn't weighing on us?'

He shrugged. 'Why not? I promise I'll take care of this. And you and I are going to relax, one way or another.'

'Okay.' But the deep crease on her forehead remained.

Cole turned south on the freeway and exited twice, looping around to make certain he wasn't being followed before settling into the two-hour drive ahead of them. He knew where he was taking her. It was a lodge on a private lake that he'd researched several years ago when things with his girlfriend at the time had gotten serious. They never made it to the lodge, though. She'd cheated on him the weekend before he planned to take her there. Cole pushed the thoughts from his mind and laced his fingers with Savannah's, doing his best to calm her.

She listened to his one-sided phone conversation as he drove. He had called someone named Norm who she believed was his boss at the FBI. It felt strange listening to him discuss her as though she wasn't seated right next to him, but she knew he was trying to help. Savannah was most interested to hear how he explained her presence in his life, but he didn't reveal much about their relationship, simply saying that Savannah from the Jacob Stone investigation was a friend of his and she needed their help.

Friend?

She was surprised to learn that this wasn't the first note Dillon had left. Apparently there had been another one left on his wind-shield a couple of weeks ago. Cole instructed Norm that it was in his desk drawer at work, inside a plastic bag, and to have it dusted for prints. Cole's voice was raised and the vein in his neck throbbed, but after a few tense moments of back and forth with Norm, Cole seemed pleased.

'Yeah, let's get this fucker. Okay, thanks Norm.' Cole ended the call and set his cell into the center console between them.

Savannah swallowed, keeping her eyes on the road. 'Everything okay?'

He reached over and took her hand. 'Yeah. It will be. Norm says he'll send someone out to pick up Dillon. The case hasn't officially been closed yet, so there's no problem with bringing him in for questioning, however loose the connection is between him and these notes. But at least they can talk to him — see what he'll say. Let him know he's still on our radar.'

'Okay.' She brought her legs up, folding them under her on the seat, and tried not to worry. Dillon was harmless. Wasn't he?

They pulled onto the one-lane private drive leading back into the woods. The sun was beginning its descent, lighting the fieldstone and timber two-story lodge in a glow of pinks, oranges and golds.

'Wow.' Savannah sat up in her seat and smiled appreciatively. 'This is beautiful.'

Cole was glad she was the first and only girl he'd brought here. And from what he remembered, the pictures online didn't do this place justice. It had a secluded, rustic feel. It was perfect.

He led her inside, their bags once again resting on his shoulder. Fleeing from danger or not, he was raised in Texas, and that meant manners, opening doors for ladies and being an all-around gentleman

When he found out that Savannah had never stayed at a hotel before, he booked them a suite, complete with a private balcony overlooking the lake. The suite was comprised of a living room with a sofa and chaise lounge chair facing a stone-hearthed fire-place, a separate bedroom sporting a king bed adorned with a fluffy white down comforter, and a large bathroom with a glass enclosed shower and separate garden tub, but it was spacious and well-appointed. He watched Savannah explore the rooms, ending her tour on the balcony. The last rays of sunlight cast off the deep blue lake. He came up behind her, caging her in against the iron railing and nuzzled her neck, breathing in her scent. She was so soft, so lovely, she provoked in him not the hardened FBI agent needing justice, but a man in need of a woman. It was easy to lose himself in her, and he almost couldn't believe he'd resisted her for so long.

The conversation with Norm had gone well, and he was confident that now that he'd bitten the bullet and involved the FBI that idiot Dillon would be taken care of. Yet he knew things were never that simple, and he felt sure he would have to come clean to Norm on Monday morning. Whatever was going to happen now was out of his control, so there was no use worrying about it. He would enjoy his secret getaway with Savannah before they were both forced to face reality and whatever came next.

They ordered in a simple dinner and ate on the couch with plates balanced on their knees. Cole had a bottle of wine delivered too, figuring they'd both need the help relaxing. Savannah did little more than pick at the food on her plate, and Cole's appetite wasn't much better. He cleared their plates and discreetly checked his phone in the kitchen. Still nothing from Norm.

He returned to living room, refilling both glasses. 'Do you want to sit out on the balcony?'

Savannah lifted her eyes to his as if the sound of his voice interrupted some private thought. 'Hm? Oh, sure.' She accepted his proffered hand and rose to her feet, dutifully following him to the cushioned bench seat on the balcony. The old-fashioned sconces provided a soft glow of flickering light, and the water lapping at the shore of the lake below was the perfect backdrop. Cole set the glasses on the table and pulled Savannah down to his lap, needing the distraction full body contact offered. He wanted to reassure her, to promise everything would be okay, but he couldn't. So he held her instead.

She giggled softly, allowing herself to be maneuvered and folded into his arms. She turned so that she was facing him and placed her palms against his cheeks.

'Why didn't you tell me about the first note?'

He swallowed and removed her hands, holding them in his lap. 'I had it handled. I didn't want you to worry unless you needed to. I just wanted to protect you as long as I could.'

'I would have rather you told me. You can't protect me from everything forever.'

'I know. I'm sorry.' He pressed a soft kiss to her lips. 'Forgive me?'

She took her time before answering, and Cole feared the other secret he'd been keeping from her was floating through her mind. 'Forgiven,' she murmured, leaning in for another kiss. She had grown more confident in initiating their physical contact, which Cole very much appreciated. His heart rate kicked up, realizing they were all alone for the night with nothing to do but enjoy their pretend romantic getaway. He deepened the kiss, nibbling her bottom lip. His hands found Savannah's ass and squeezed, hauling her in closer to his groin. A groan of frustration bubbled deep in her throat and she clutched at his biceps. It was as if they both needed to be closer. Now.

He stood, lifting her as he headed inside. She wrapped her legs around his waist and her arms around his neck, still not breaking their kiss. Not bothering to turn on the bedroom light, Cole laid Savannah on the bed, leaning over to plant a tender kiss on her mouth before he stood to admire her, sprawled out against the bed. Her dark hair was a halo of loose curls on the pillow, and her arms reluctantly dropped from his neck, as if unwilling to release him.

'God you're perfect,' he breathed. Her eyes remained locked on his, refusing to look away, refusing to break their unspoken connection. 'Do you know how hard it was to resist you?'

'You hardly noticed me. Do you know how many times I wandered around your room in just my panties trying to tempt you?'

'Yes. Forty-seven.'

'What?' she chuckled.

'Kidding. I didn't keep count. But you're wrong about me not noticing. I noticed every damn time.' And so did his dick. He'd had a perpetual case of blue balls practically since the day she moved in. 'You're amazing, Savannah. Beautiful, smart, loving. How could I not notice you?' *And fall for you?*

A satisfied little smile tugged at her mouth and he knew he needed her, needed to show her that she was his. His hands found his belt and quickly unlatched the buckle before moving to the button and zipper. Savannah followed his movements, eyes wide and curious. He yanked his T-shirt over his head and let it fall to the floor. Savannah squirmed on the bed, still watching him. When he pushed his jeans and boxers down his hips, she licked her lips. And when his hand caught and lazily stroked his length, she exhaled slowly.

'Cole…' Her voice was a broken plea in the otherwise silent room.

'Yeah babe?' He continued his slow movements along his engorged shaft, his hand gripping the base and sliding up over the sensitive tip.

Her gaze darted down to his groin and she bit her lip again. 'Did you…um, do that…when you thought about me?'

Her question surprised him. He hadn't expected her to have the balls to ask something like that. 'Yeah. I did.' *Often. Too often.*

She sucked in a breath and reached for his cock, gripping her hand tightly around his. Cole's movements stilled momentarily, appreciating the feel of her warmth. But the desire reflected in her eyes forced his hand to slide up and over his head once again. He pulled in a shuddering breath. Introducing her soft hand to the mix upped the pleasure quota significantly. He let her grip him, and he guided her— nice and slow. 'Savannah,' he whispered.

Her eyes flashed to his. 'How often did you…do this before we slept together?'

Fuck. Was she really asking him how often he masturbated? He couldn't answer that question. 'Enough.' *Daily.*

She smiled, seemingly satisfied with his non-answer. Savannah's free hand fumbled with the button on her jeans and Cole abandoned his show to help. Once her jeans and panties were off, he took a moment to just admire her. She was so lovely—soft where a woman should be soft, curvy and delicate at the same time. God, even her feet were fucking pretty. He wanted to bow and worship her body like she deserved, but she pulled off her shirt and scrambled across the bed to him. She perched on her knees on the edge of the bed, wrapping her arms around his neck and lifting her chin to kiss him. Her chest pressed against his, warm and molding to his form. Her warm tongue slid against his and he was lost to all rational thought. He needed to taste her, to be inside her, to own her…

'Cole?' Savannah broke away from the kiss, her hands planted on his chest, roaming over his tensed abs.

'Yeah?' He stroked a single fingertip along her cheek. 'What is it?'

'I don't want this to end. Me and you.'

His shoulders relaxed. He loved her bravery, her honesty. And he'd been slightly worried she was going to tell him this wasn't a good idea. 'Me neither.' It was the absolute truth. He wasn't willing to lose Savannah. Whatever it took. He couldn't explain how or why, but she belonged with him. He ignored the tightening in his chest, refusing to acknowledge how he could possibly have a future with Savannah with his past still firmly gripping him.

194

He pushed her shoulders back, and she fell against the bed, giggling. But her laughter died when he pulled her thighs apart and positioned himself at her entrance. Fuck using a condom. He needed her too bad. They'd have to risk it, something he'd never done before. But realizing the decision wasn't just his, he stopped just short of entering her. He placed a palm flat on her stomach. 'I want to feel you without a condom …are you okay with that?'

Savannah's expression pinched for just a moment, as if she was counting the days. 'It's fine,' she murmured. She gripped his hips and tugged him forward. Cole obliged, taking the base of his shaft and guiding himself into her impossibly tight channel.

There was nothing between them. New sensations flooded Cole's system. 'Fuck, Savannah,' he growled as she squeezed around him. Normally he found reaching his release difficult, sometimes taking close to an hour — but not with Savannah. Being inside her was an entirely new experience. He was like a teenager trying not to come too soon. Savannah's parted lips and flushed chest only spurred him on, and when she released a series of tiny high-pitched moans, he nearly came undone. His fingers gripped the flesh of her hips as he drove in faster, seeking his release.

Savannah's hands clutched at his hands, his stomach, anywhere she could reach as her moans built. 'Cole!' She groaned a final time in an incoherent tumble of sounds and tossed her head back against the pillow, her back arching as she came.

His own orgasm hit him like a punch to the gut, crashing against him, causing his legs to nearly give out as his body tensed and jerked. He fell on top of Savannah, finding her mouth for several damp kisses as he emptied himself into her in a series hot bursts.

Chapter 31

The situation with Dillon had been handled better than he could have hoped. The new job he'd left the compound to pursue was dealing drugs. *Moron*. When Norm sent the guys out to pick him up for questioning, they found him with enough marijuana in his car to lock him up for a while. That didn't mean his obsession with Savannah had ended, but at least he wouldn't be able to get anywhere near her for a while. And when the time came, Cole would be there to keep her safe. Her hand squeezed his and Cole smiled at the gorgeous girl next to him.

'Almost home,' he said. *Home*. It had felt more like a home since Savannah had moved in.

'I can't wait to see Cuddles.'

Cole pulled into the parking lot of his condo complex and his eyes couldn't quite process the scene before him. Abbie was standing on the sidewalk, her arms folded over her chest watching his SUV approach. His eyes flashed to the clock on his dash. *Fuck*. A curse tore from his chest at the sight of her. He had missed their Sunday appointment and now she was here. Here. At his home. Savannah's home.

He considered gunning the engine and tearing out of the parking lot, but he didn't have the strength to lie to Savannah anymore. His past was here—staring down his future, shattering his heart into a million tiny pieces.

*

Watching the fragile dark-haired girl run to Cole and throw herself into his arms knocked the wind from Savannah's chest. She placed a hand against the hood of the Tahoe to prop herself up. Cole placed his hands on the girl's shoulders, gently moving her away from his body. His eyes flashed to Savannah's, panic written all over his face.

'This is Abbie,' he said, but didn't offer anything more.

Savannah hated the familiarity between them — the way Abbie's body tilted towards his and the way his fingers had knowingly soothed down her arms as he moved her away. Abbie turned to look Savannah over, her bright blue eyes burning with curiosity. Abbie was thin and pretty with delicate features. She was dressed casually in a pair of worn jeans and flowing pink top that was too large on her tiny frame.

'Is this her?' Abbie asked him.

Cole nodded. 'This is Savannah.'

Abbie's gaze found Cole's, seeking permission, before she thrust a hand out to Savannah. There were scars marring her inner wrist and when Savannah's gaze lingered on the puckered white flesh, Abbie pulled her hand back and stuffed it into her pocket. 'Hi,' Abbie offered, smiling carefully. 'Cole's told me a lot about you.'

Savannah remained speechless. She felt sick. Humiliated.

Abbie turned back to Cole, her expression softening. 'You didn't show up today, I got worried. Are you mad I came here?' She lifted a hand to his cheek, but Cole caught her wrist.

His eyes flashed back to Savannah. He flinched, opened his mouth, then closed it again. There was nothing he could say. Savannah's skin tingled as awareness flooded her. This was who he spent every Sunday with?

The scars on Abbie's wrists, the needy way she looked at Cole like a child separated from its mother, it struck her like a thump to

197

the head — all the times he'd looked at her like she was unstable, fear in his eyes that she'd break down and lose it. Did he have some strange calling to save needy girls? She wasn't like this girl, and she resented his careful watch even more now, because it meant memories of Abbie were still right there at the surface.

He turned to Savannah, handing her the keys. 'Can you ah, give us a minute?'

Savannah wished she had some place to go — anywhere but inside his house. She wanted to flee somewhere far away from here, but she accepted the keys and ventured up the stairs, too stunned to cry, too shocked to process what she'd just learned.

Cole had gotten rid of Abbie and ventured inside to talk to Savannah. He needed to come clean about everything—all of it—not spare any of the details.

He found Savannah hiding underneath the comforter in the guest room, whispering to a squirming mass under there with her. He'd let her down, and she'd turned to the dog for comfort. It was a sobering thought.

He sat quietly on the edge of the bed. Her whispering stopped as soon as the mattress dipped with his weight.

'You don't have to talk to me. Just listen, okay?' He released a heavy sigh, knowing this conversation was long overdue. 'I first met Abbie just after college. She was broken—a project for me— someone I could focus my energy on since I'd been so powerless to prevent my parents' deaths.' Cole scrubbed his hands over his face. It was harder than he thought it'd be admitting all this out loud. 'Abbie was a cutter, which I'd found out later. She was abused as a child. She was a wreck when we first started dating. Our relation-ship was full of self-doubt, jealousy, and at times intense passion.' Cole wished he could see Savannah's expression, get a sense of how she was taking it. But the damned comforter covered her from head to toe. 'We dated for two years, and eventually she got better. Later I came to realize that I wasn't in love with her — I'd only been in love with the idea of saving someone. Once Abbie was well, the intensity behind our relationship all but disappeared.'

Savannah pushed the covers down, her face coming into view. He expected her to be crying, but her eyes were dry, curiously gazing at him; her face relaxed.

'I tried numerous times to break things off with her, but Abbie would freak out. So I'd stay. We hung on that way for another six months until I couldn't endure the cycle anymore. I ended it for good.'

Cuddles squirmed her way out from the blankets and licked Savannah's nose. She folded the puppy along her side and mumbled, 'Keep talking.'

'I broke up with her and thought I was done. Of course, I hadn't expected Abbie to try and end her life. But that same day, she'd slashed her wrists. Her roommate found her and rushed her to the hospital, and called me on the way. When I saw how truly broken she was—pale and weak in that hospital bed, tubes running everywhere—I knew it was my fault. I'd vowed to save her, and now she was worse off than she'd ever been. Because of me. It ate away at me, and I knew I couldn't run again. Not when she was so incredibly fragile.

'Abbie stayed at the hospital for a few days, she'd lost a lot of blood, and when she recovered physically from the suicide attempt, she was taken to a psychiatric facility. She stayed there for over a year before she moved back into her own apartment, just down the road from here. We never rekindled our romantic relationship, but all this time—close to five years now—I've faithfully visited her every week, as a friend, and as her security blanket, I guess.'

Tears began to fill Savannah's eyes as she sat stoically.

'Savannah? Please say something,' he begged.

Savannah grabbed her car keys and left.

Chapter 32

'What the fuck did you do?' Marissa's voice shrilled from the phone as he sat at the bar.

'What are you talking about?' In Cole's drunken state, it took him a second to comprehend the anger in her voice. *Oh. Fuck.*

Her voice dropped to a whisper, 'Why is Savannah camped out in my bathroom?'

'Cole? Answer me, dammit,' Marissa shrilled.

He dragged the phone away from his ear, closing his eyes. Maybe those six Jack and Cokes he'd knocked back weren't the best idea. 'I fucked up, okay? Is that what you want to hear, Rissa?'

She stayed silent.

'Is she really in the bathroom crying?'

'Of course she is. She told me, well as best she could, about Abbie. Goddammit Cole, that girl was a wreck. I had no idea you were still seeing her all these years.'

'Yeah…well…' He scrubbed a hand over the back of his neck. Marissa had met Abbie years ago when they were dating. Liam's questioning gaze met his, silently asking him if he wanted another drink. Cole waved him away. 'Pretty fucking stupid of me, huh?' He had put his own life on hold, barely dated, barely did anything but work and faithfully visit Abbie every Sunday, simply because he knew it cheered her up. And then when the whole Dillon thing cropped up, he'd completely forgotten about her. He'd never forgotten a Sunday before. Never.

Marissa sighed. 'I didn't say that. But Jesus, Cole, you can't take sole responsibility for saving every girl you meet. And Savannah didn't need saving. She just needed your love.'

'Don't tell me what Savannah needed. I know what she needs,' he said, anger bubbling up inside him. He gripped the bar until his knuckles turned white, avoiding the urge to hit something.

'Listen, I've got to go. Savannah's just come out.'

'Let me talk to —' The phone went dead.

Fuck! He slammed his phone down onto the bar in front of him. Liam sauntered over, eyeing him with caution. 'Was that Savannah?'

'No.' He didn't mention it was Marissa, because every time he brought Marissa's name up lately, Liam wanted to play twenty questions with him. He was almost ready to tell him it was fine — he could ask his sister out—but figured he'd make him suffer a little more. Cole tried to stand, gripping the bar for support.

Liam shook his head. 'I'll call you a cab. Take your drunk ass home.'

'I'm not drunk,' Cole slurred. Okay, maybe a little. 'Yeah, all right,' he conceded.

Liam slapped Cole's shoulder, resting his hand there. 'I think you're in love with her, bro.'

Not Fucking Helpful. Why did everyone keep saying it? Cole shrugged out of his grip and headed outside to wait for his cab.

He made his way upstairs, gripping the wall for support. He tried the door knob, found it unlocked and went inside. Marissa and Savannah were huddled around her dining room table. Seeing Savannah's puffy, red eyes was like a fist to his gut. All the air was sucked from his lungs. He'd done that to her.

'Cole! You shouldn't have been driving!' Marissa screamed, jumping up to punch him on the shoulder. Neither had any

Kendall Ryan

tolerance for drunk drivers after the way their parents were taken from them.

He held up his hands in surrender. 'I took a cab, relax.' He stepped around Marissa, heading straight for Savannah like she was a light at the end of a tunnel, his beacon in the darkness. He'd been trying to save everyone, yet Savannah had been the one to teach him. Her compassion, her genuine nature continued to level him. She was all he needed. And he'd been so wrong. She didn't need saving — *he* did. He knew with certainly, he'd grovel, beg, and promise her the world, if she'd only hear him out.

Savannah watched him with guarded eyes, drawing a shaky breath.

'We need to talk.' His voice was a coarse, broken plea in the room.

Marissa stepped between them, her hands planting themselves on her hips. 'I don't think that's a good idea right now. You're drunk, Cole.'

Without removing his eyes from Savannah's, he muttered the only word he could think of. 'Please.'

Savannah merely nodded and followed him back to Marissa's office. She sunk down into the leather office chair. Cole leaned against the door frame, hating that he no longer had the right to pull her into his arms. Hating that she no longer needed him for comfort, and that he was the source of her pain.

'Savannah, I'm sorry, so sorry that I kept Abbie from you.'

She held up her hand. 'Don't say her name.'

Shit. His shaky legs gave out and he slid down the wall to sit on the floor. God, he needed to think. How did he ask for a second chance from the girl who meant everything to him?

'What am I supposed to do now?' Savannah asked, brokenly. 'I feel like a total fool. You humiliated me, Cole. I thought we had something special…I had no idea you were off…' She stopped short, sucking in a deep breath and holding it. He could see that she was trying not to cry again. He hated himself even more.

He looked up. Sadness blazed in her green eyes, made all the more brilliant from her tears. 'We do have something special. Don't give up on me, Savannah. I fucked up big time, and I know that. I thought I was doing the right thing continuing to see Ab- *her*, but you're right, okay?'

A single tear escaped and rolled down her cheek. Cole crossed the room on his knees, taking her face in his hands and wiping away the dampness with his thumbs. 'I'm so fucking sorry, Savannah. Please don't cry. Please, baby.' He was not above begging if that's what it took.

'You lied. You left every Sunday to see her while I waited for you.'

The pain in her features crashed through him. What if she couldn't forgive him? He would do anything; spend his life trying to re-earn her trust.

'I know. And I shouldn't have kept that from you, I was just so torn up over what to do.' His heart thumped erratically in his chest. 'But you're the one I love, Savannah.'

Her eyes widened. 'You're drunk. Don't say that.'

'I am drunk, but you think I've just now realized that I love you? I started falling the moment I saw you. Then you came home with me and even though you should have been a mess, you were taking charge in my kitchen, cooking for me, taking care of me when I had the flu, and the first time we made love?' He fought off a shiver at the memory. 'It's never been like that for me before. I'm in love with you, Savannah. Hopelessly and completely. You own me, baby.'

Her mouth tugged into a small grin and she swallowed. He ached to kiss her, but he didn't know if that was allowed. He'd never had to grovel before. He'd always been the one to cut out on relationships, never the one seeking.

'And I explained to Abbie that we both needed to move on. I'm not going to see her anymore. I'm yours. You own me, Savannah.

You always have.' Suddenly it seemed very fitting that he was on his knees before her.

Two heartbeats passed and still Savannah remained quiet, her eyes locked on his. She brought her hand to his stubble-covered cheek and held him there. 'I knew I was falling in love with you, but then when I saw…*her*… and found out you'd been seeing her behind my back this whole time, it destroyed me.'

'No.' He placed his hand over hers, holding it to his skin. 'Don't say that. I can't handle that I hurt you. Please let me fix it.'

'Let me finish.' She straightened her shoulders, seeming to draw composure from the small move. 'I've only known you a short time, but you wedged yourself into my heart. You became everything to me. My entire life before you fell away, and I had the chance to be me, to become who I wanted. You helped me, without any selfish motivation of your own. And I probably shouldn't, but I trust you. I've always trusted you, right from the very beginning. If you say you're done seeing her —then I believe you. But don't you dare break my trust again.'

He grinned, liking the strength he heard in her voice. Seeing her growth and confidence was sexy. He brushed her hair back from her tear-streaked face, aching to kiss her, to take away all her pain. *Stop thinking with your dick, asshole.* 'I hate that I made you cry. I hate seeing you like this,' he admitted, his thumb tracing gentle circles over her cheek.

Savannah's gaze intensified. 'Even though I'd be heartbroken without you, Cole, I wouldn't be broken like Abbie was. I'm not her. I don't want you walking on eggshells around me, or afraid to tell me things because I might not like them. If we're going to have a relationship, it has to be on equal footing. I want to be your partner, not your project.'

Cole remained silent for several long seconds, working to understand her plea. 'I know you're not her. You're an amazing, beautiful, strong woman who has complete command over my heart, hell my entire body. I've never loved anyone like this, Savannah. You're everything to me, and I wanted to shield you from all the fucked up shit from my past. I don't want a project either, but I am always going to be your protector. That's just how I'm wired, babe. I won't let anyone or anything hurt you.'

She nodded. 'Okay. I just wanted you to understand. You can't break me like that, so don't hold things back from me. If this is going to work, you have to communicate with me — with complete honesty.'

'I can do that.' He smiled, and Savannah's gaze wandered to his mouth. 'Babe?' he asked, leaning closer, his own eyes flicking between hers and her lips.

'Yeah?' Her voice was just as breathless as he felt. The effect of her so close it was dizzying, intoxicating.

'If you want complete honesty…I need to kiss you now.'

Savannah's tongue dampened her bottom lip and Cole leaned forward, sealing their mouths together in a passionate kiss.

Cole's mouth felt good. Too good. Savannah was lost to pleasure, sensation. Her brain struggling to give up control to her body.

A series of firm knocks rained against the door. 'Um, Cole?' Marissa's muffled voice came from the hallway.

Crap!

Cole lifted his head. 'We're busy,' he called toward the door.

Savannah's eyes darted to the door knob, trying to remember if they'd locked it, not that she expected Marissa to barge in or anything. But God, she couldn't imagine anything more embarrassing. Her jeans were around her ankles and Cole's face was buried…well, somewhere good.

Marissa knocked again, more insistently this time. 'I'm glad to hear you're um…making up….and I don't care that you're drunk and in my apartment. I do care, however, that you're fucking loud enough to wake half my building. Come on, I'm driving you guys home,' she called.

Heat flamed in her cheeks. *Shit*. Had she been too loud?

'Just give us a few more minutes,' Cole growled.

Savannah moved to get up, trying to adjust her clothes, but Cole held her in place. 'Stay.'

Her eyes searched his. 'We can't…we should go.'

He shook his head and bent to nibble on her inner thigh. 'We will. But I want to make you come first,' he whispered. His breath rushed over her core, and a wave of dampness surged between her legs.

'Cole…' she pleaded, brokenly.

'Shh.' He moved her panties to the side once again so her swollen pink flesh was on full display. 'Let me finish taking care of you, then we'll go.' His mouth covered her sensitive flesh and, tossing all manners aside, he ate at her greedily, licking and suckling until she was writhing again. She groaned loudly and Cole's hand came up and clamped down over her mouth, his eyes watching her reaction as his mouth continued its greedy display.

She was nearly sliding off the leather chair, but the pressure of Cole's face between her legs held her in place. She should have felt embarrassed, overwhelmed by his dominance, but instead she just felt loved. Incredibly cherished and loved. And apparently delicious.

He focused in on her sensitive flesh, finding a rhythm that destroyed all thoughts of Marissa waiting on the other side of the door.

She came hard and fast, her hips lifting from the chair, her hands fisting in Cole's hair.

Her body shuddered with the violence of her release and when she opened her eyes, she was surprised to find herself in Cole's arms. He'd lifted her from the chair and was holding her against his body, her feet dangling several inches from the floor. He kissed her mouth, and she tasted her own arousal, and liquor, and Cole. Her eyes drifted closed again in sated satisfaction.

He let her slide down his body until her feet reached the floor. Cole took her face in his hands, pressing a final kiss to her mouth. 'I love you.'

'I love you too.' It felt so good to finally say it to him, and even better to hear him say those words.

'Can I take you home?'

Home. The word rolled easily from his tongue and made her feel even more complete and happy than she thought possible.

Suddenly becoming aware of the large bulge in his jeans, she gestured to his lap. 'What about you?'

He winced as he adjusted his staining erection. 'I'll live.'

Chapter 33

When they got home, Cole stopped Savannah from going inside and lifted her in his arms to carry her across the threshold. It reminded him of the first day he'd met her. He'd taken her in his arms then too. It'd just felt right. It still did. There was something so familiar about her, like she was made to be his. He carried through the darkened rooms and laid her on his bed—their bed—and set about removing her clothes piece by piece. His erection hadn't gone down since their encounter in Marissa's office over thirty minutes ago. He knew he would need her twice before he found relief. The first time would be hard and fast, the second time slower and more controlled.

He slid her panties—still damp from her earlier release—down her legs and discarded them on the floor before moving to his own belt buckle. Savannah watched with wide eyes as he removed every last stich of clothing between them. She looked at his engorged cock and then at his right hand. He knew what she wanted, and he obliged, gripping himself and stroking lightly. She licked her lips, slowly tracing them with her tongue. Fuck, he needed to be inside her. Like yesterday. He was already leaking pre-come and his balls ached.

She rolled to her side, her dark hair spilling across the pillow and reached a hand toward him, her eyes still watching everything. She caressed his thigh, his abs, fingernails scraping against his

208

skin. He continued his slow lazy strokes for his incredibly sexy audience of one. If he could get her to touch herself for him, fuck, that would probably be his undoing. Her hand continued lightly brushing his skin, deliciously close to where his throbbing dick begged for her attention.

With one hand still wrapped firmly around himself, he took her hand in his and brought it to the juncture between her legs. Savannah's eyes widened, but she went with it, letting one knee drop open. Knowing how sweet she tasted, how wet he could get her, the sexy moans she made in the back of her throat tempted him to pleasure her again; but reading her body, he knew she needed something more. He pressed one finger inside her, watching his middle finger disappear to the second knuckle and he was rewarded with a satisfied groan from Savannah. He retracted his hand, encouraging her to take over. Savannah's hand stilled as if this was unexplored territory. *She'd never touched herself before?*

She took a deep breath, her chest rising, and used her fingers to rub and explore. This moment was more meaningful than just the two of them touching, discovering. He knew Savannah was opening herself up to him, to everything, to life. She was done being sheltered and feeling ashamed for what she wanted. She wanted to feel—every little thing—all that life had to offer. His heart surged knowing she wouldn't hold back from him.

Watching her fingers, tipped in pink nail polish rubbing against her tender flesh, circling that that little nub near the top sent a rush of heat through him, producing another drop of fluid to leak from his cock. He bit back a groan. 'Savannah…' he breathed, bending to kiss her, their mouths desperately moving against one another in a flash of gliding wet tongues and barely contained moans. 'I need to be inside you, baby.'

*

He joined her on the bed, pulling her hips closer, causing her entire body to slide down the bed towards him. She placed a hand on his forearm to stop him.

'Can we…try a different position?' Without waiting for him to answer, she rolled to her stomach, displaying that fine little ass for him. *Fuck. Was this girl made just for him?*

'Anything you want, babe,' he said in a low whisper since all the air was sucked from his lungs at the sight of her. He trailed a hand down her back, lightly tickling, and Savannah squirmed in the most enticing way. He straddled her tightly closed thighs, and Savannah turned her face on the pillow to watch him. Dropping a kiss to her mouth, her chin, her shoulder, he took himself in hand and gently stoked his length as it rested between her buttocks.

She watched him with a hooded gaze, still squirming beneath him. 'Do I need to open my legs?' she asked, blinking up at him.

He supposed it was an honest question, but no, he could reach all of her delicious parts just like this, and she'd feel even tighter with her legs clamped together. 'No, baby. Stay just like you are.'

She swallowed and nodded.

The anticipation of being inside her nearly killed him. He gripped her hips, his fingers digging into her flesh, his thumbs parting her cheeks, so he could see below to her beautiful little pussy. His cock was rock hard and sliding along her ass, as if seeking the heat between her legs. Her head remained turned on the pillow so she could watch him. He met her eyes and continued rubbing himself along the crease of her ass. Savannah flinched at the new sensations, and he leaned down to drop a kiss to her mouth. He wouldn't take her there. Wouldn't do anything she wasn't ready for. 'Do you trust me?'

She nodded, her lips parted and breaths escaping in quick succession.

He inched forward, watching as the head of his cock disappeared into her slick, pink flesh. Her hips lifted to meet his next thrust, sending him deeper. A surge of pleasure flooded his system, prickling against his spine and a low guttural groan escaped his throat. His placed a hand on her lower back, keeping her still. If she was going to work her ass against him like that, he'd lose it.

Holding her hips steady, he plunged into her, again and again, his pace quickening as the pleasure became too much. Savannah was writhing and wiggling underneath him, and each time he thrust forward, burying himself deep, she let out a small cry. *Fuck, she was tight.*

He gripped her ass in his hands, pushing into her faster, harder, until both their cries of pleasure were loud and uncontained. At the last moment, he pulled himself free from her body, and used his hand to wring the pleasure exploding inside him onto her buttocks, covering her, marking her. She was his. Now and forever.

She lay still and breathing hard while Cole scurried into the bathroom, returning with a warm washcloth to clean her. Once she was cleaned of the evidence of their love-making, he lay down beside her, tugging her close and buried his face in the crook of her neck. They remained that way, their hearts pounding in a matched rhythm for several minutes, neither of them willing to break the spell.

Cole eventually eased from the warm cocoon of her body, so that he could look at her.

A smile passed Savannah's lips and she brought her hand to his hair, trying to smooth the disheveled strands. 'Hi.'

'Hi.' He pressed a kiss to her mouth.

She blinked up at him. 'You were drunk.'

'I know.' He'd been drunk off his ass, but Savannah's presence and that powerful orgasm had sobered him completely. He'd been drinking to numb the pain, a deep searing pain that a few hours ago seemed impossible to overcome. 'I thought I'd lost you.' He stoked her hair back from her face, amazed that she was here in

211

his arms again. 'I won't do anything to fuck this up. I promise you, Savannah.'

She stayed quiet, letting him hold her. He waited for her to barrage him with questions, but he supposed after his admission of the entire story with Abbie earlier, and now sharing her body with him….did that mean he was forgiven?

'Does this mean you're giving me another chance?'

She pressed a kiss to his throat. 'Possibly.' Her voice was coy, but her arms around him felt strong and sure.

'I love you so much, baby.'

'I love you too, Cole.'

Epilogue

Three Years Later

Cole's hands captured her hips, pulling her in snuggly so her back rested against his chest. 'Enjoying the party?' his breath whispered across her ear, sending fine tingles skittering down her spine.

Things had been a little awkward for them both at the first work function Savannah attended, but now their relationship wasn't really much of a *thing* anymore. Only a few people knew how they first met, and even though Cole's boss Norm was one of them, he'd turned a blind eye, taking on a *don't ask, don't tell* philosophy. Cole had tried to explain things to him once, but Norm had waved him off, saying what he didn't know wouldn't hurt him. Savannah had been to countless work functions with him since then, and she was pleased to be accepted into the fold with the other wives. She was younger than most, sure, but she'd always been mature for her age, so it really wasn't an issue.

'Baby?' Cole was still waiting for her response.

She leaned against him. Her high heels were pinching her feet, and her panty hose cutting were into her sides, but she smiled and patted his hand resting on her belly. 'I'm fine, love.'

'And my little daughter… how's she? Still turning somersaults in there?' His hand smoothed over the satin of her dress to caress her swollen belly.

'She had the hiccups after I ate that spicy crab dip, but she seems fine now.'

He chuckled against her skin and pressed a damp kiss against the back of her neck. That was one benefit of having her hair twisted up in a knot. With his hand still on her belly, he spoke softly in her ear. 'I'll give you a massage when we get home if you like.'

While other men celebrated nine months of having a designated driver on hand, Cole hadn't had so much as a single drink during her pregnancy. He was a saint—attending every doctor's appointment, reading all the baby books and pretty much waiting on her hand and foot. She'd had a stern talking to him after he made her breakfast in bed for a month straight and tried to carry her from room to room. If he'd been protective and attentive before her pregnancy, he was psychotic mother hen during it.

He'd calmed down a little since then, but still insisted on massaging her shoulders, or her feet at the end of a long day. Savannah didn't complain. Especially since the massages usually led to more. Cole had been hesitant at first about making love to her, limiting their activities to oral sex or extended make out sessions like they were teenagers, until she'd gotten the doctor to tell Cole it was safe. Now they were making up for lost time, for which Savannah was grateful. She found pregnancy made her highly orgasmic.

The music changed and softened and Cole swayed with her in his arms. The pregnancy made him deliriously happy — her too, but she'd always wanted children —he hadn't been so sure when they first met. But with Cole's thirtieth birthday drawing closer, he became more and more persistent about the idea of becoming a father. They'd been tempting fate without condoms or birth control for the last couple of years anyway, but suddenly Savannah noticed he was asking about her cycles, talking about timing sex, coming home from the drug store with boxes of pregnancy tests.

She still smiled at the memory. She'd never pictured FBI agent, alpha-male Cole to be modeling baby carriers in the store, or checking the thread-count on baby blankets. All the many sides of this man surprised her. She loved the way he still made her feel like the most gorgeous woman in the room, instead of the beached whale she felt like a in the wine-colored evening gown stretching across her growing belly.

'How are your feet holding up?' he asked, speaking low near her ear once again.

Cole knew her feet often swelled to the size of balloons by the end of the night — and that was when they weren't stuffed into stiletto heels.

'I'm looking forward to that massage later.' She didn't want to complain, knowing he'd insist on whisking her away.

He lifted the hem of her floor-length gown. Yep, swollen like sausages. 'Why didn't you say something?'

She shrugged. She hadn't wanted him to miss the part of the reception where he was receiving special honors for his work on a critical case he'd helped solve.

Without another word Cole ushered her through the crowd, nodding once to Norm on their way toward the exit. He handed the valet their ticket and soon they were seated in the darkened cab of his SUV, Cole's hand resting on her knee. The infant seat was already installed in the backseat, a full two months before her due date.

Once inside, Cuddles greeted them in her customary manner — providing wet kisses to Savannah, and nipping at Cole's ankles. They both chuckled and Cole bent and scooped Cuddles into his arms. 'I'll take her out. Go get comfortable.' He pressed a kiss to her mouth before heading out the door.

Savannah shed her dress and the offensive undergarments cutting off her circulation before stretching out on the bed. Cole returned a few minutes later, and she felt his presence before she saw him. He stood in the doorway just watching her. He still held the power to heat her skin with a single look and she was pretty sure if she was wearing panties, they'd be damp. 'Are you going to join me, or are you going to stand there staring all night?'

His expression changed, breaking into an easy smile. 'I want to remember you like this.' He crossed the room toward her. 'You are so beautiful, Savannah.'

He sat beside her stretched out form, gently taking her feet into his lap, kneading one foot, working his thumbs up the arch.

'Did you ever think we'd be married and have a baby on the way?'

He switched his treatment to her other foot, his knuckles pressing into her instep. 'You mean when we first met?'

She nodded, fighting off the chill bumps his talented hands were sending up her body.

'No, but only because I wouldn't let myself picture it. I was trying my damnedest to resist you. Of course you were beautiful, but then you were so unexpected too, caring, giving and sweet.'

'And eventually you stopped resisting me,' she commented.

'Yes, I did. Thank fucking God,' he returned, leaning over her to drop a tender kiss to her mouth.

Her fingers found the top button of his dress shirt, and began working to unbutton them. 'Skin,' she mumbled against his mouth. 'I need to feel your skin.'

He obliged, quickly losing his shirt, dress pants, socks, and pushing his boxers down his thighs to lie next to her fully nude.

As Cole's body wrapped around hers, Savannah gave a contented sigh and allowed him to hold her. Their heartbeats thumped together as if acknowledging the courage it took to pursue what was in their hearts. Life had unfolded in unexpected ways, the events of the last few years irrevocably drawing them together. His large hands smoothed over her hips, down to her backside to draw her closer. His touch no longer set off sparks against her skin, but always made her feel safe, loved and cherished.

'I love you, Cole Fletcher,' Savannah murmured into his warm chest.

'I love you more, baby.'

She rested her head against his firm chest and closed her eyes, feeling safe and secure in his arms. She was home.

Acknowledgements

Once again, a giant thank you to my readers. None of this would be possible without your support. I love connecting with you on Facebook, Twitter, and GoodReads. Let's hang out...Virtually!

Fact: I have the sexiest critique partners on the planet. Thank you for your time and thoughtful critiques: Kylie, Madison, Denise, Sali and Jenny. Smooches, gals. To fellow author Charlie Evans. Thank you for your enthusiasm and advice. (I loved that you called dibs on Cole within the first chapter.)

Thank you to my dear husband for putting up with my crazy, for being my own personal naughty word thesaurus, and for encouraging me every step of the way. Best. Husband. Ever. Thanks also to my puppy babies, Lucy and Sugar. Mommy loves you, now stop chewing on that shoe!